The Time Traveler's Boyfriend

Annabelle Costa

DEV
LOVE
PRESS

THE TIME TRAVELER'S BOYFRIEND

A book by Dev Love Press, published by arrangement with the author

PRINTING HISTORY
Dev Love Press Edition/February 2014

Copyright © 2014 by Dev Love Press, LLC.
Proofread by Sarah Barbour of Aeroplane Media
Cover design by Libby Wight

Visit our website at **www.devlovepress.com**

ISBN: *978-0-9858263-5-2*

WHY ARE YOU TRAVELING BACK IN TIME?

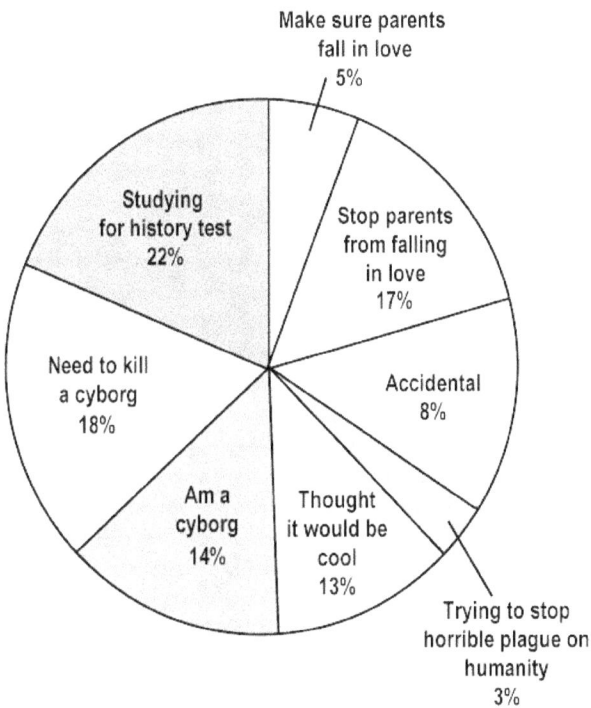

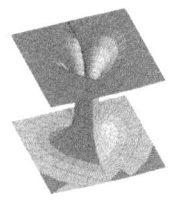

One

Tick tock, tick tock, tick tock…

Do you hear that ticking noise? I swear to God, it's like I'm going crazy, but I hear something ticking. And no, it's not my biological clock, thank you very much. Yes, my biological clock is ticking (I know, Mom), but it's not *audibly* ticking. Like, I don't walk down the street and hear it. Nobody says, "Hey, what's that noise? Is that your *ovaries*?"

So no, the source of the ticking is something less abstract than my thirty-six-year-old eggs.

Tick tock, tick tock, tick tock …

I look around the entrance to my boyfriend Adam's brownstone, located on the Upper West Side in Manhattan. Yes, it's a great location, and no, I'm not dating him for that reason. There are five steps to the main doorway, and the stairs have that appearance of dirt having been ground into them over a period of decades. I can't help but notice that some thoughtless person has stuck a wad of gum on the railing — if Adam sees it, he'll be pissed. But it's unlikely he'll notice it. He lives on the ground level, which has a separate entrance, and he rents out the upper levels to tenants that he has little to no interaction with.

Adam is not much for small talk with the neighbors.

In any case, I am absolutely certain something around here is ticking and I'll be damned if I don't figure out what it is. You can't be too careful these days, what with terrorism and all. Although I've heard that modern bombs actually don't tick. They vibrate. So it's easy to get them confused with … well, do I really need to complete that sentence? We all know what vibrates.

I do a three-hundred-and-sixty-degree turn, keeping my eyes focused on finding anything unusual, and I don't see anything, until… yes!

I almost missed it because it's huddled in some shrubbery. Mrs. Jessup on the second level thinks she has a green thumb and Adam has indulged her by allowing her to plant a miniscule garden just adjacent to the steps. Ordinarily, the garden is just grass, tulips and azaleas, but today there's something else in the little garden. Something alive.

It's a rabbit.

A rabbit. Okay, that's weird.

Let me be clear about something here. We're not in suburbia. We're not in some forest where rabbits frolic freely and play with their friends the deer and the antelope. You don't generally see rabbits wandering around the Upper West Side. Especially a rabbit like this one, which is white as snow aside from a tiny little black patch on its back and has a ticking timepiece hanging around his neck. No, this definitely isn't a wild rabbit. And I'll bet anything that its presence has something to do with Adam.

Tick tock, tick tock, tick tock …

I bend down near the little trembling rabbit, holding out my hand. See, Adam? I can be maternal. The rabbit looks at me curiously, sniffs with its little adorable nose, and then cowers in the corner like I'm the hunter in *Bambi*.

Okay, I'm not great with animals.

I straighten up, cocking my head at Adam's window to see if he's watching me. Maybe this is some kind of psychological experiment he's doing and the whole thing is being filmed and will probably end up published in the *Journal of Complicated Science*. Knowing Adam, it's got to be some kind of experiment. I just can't imagine what.

Question: Why is there a white rabbit with a clock around its neck outside my mad scientist boyfriend's house?

a) Rabbit is looking for Alice and is very, very late.

b) Adam tossed the rabbit out the window to see if time flies.

c) Rabbit is some kind of cyborg created to destroy humanity before we destroy the planet.

I turn back to get a closer look at the rabbit and now it's gone. Apparently, the little bugger ran off the second I turned my head. He isn't even close anymore because the ticking has completely stopped. And as for me, I'm left staring at the steps of the brownstone, wondering if I've completely lost my mind.

***

"A what?"

Adam denies the whole thing. There was no rabbit, he claims. I just plain imagined it.

I am apparently that crazy.

"A white rabbit," I say again through gritted teeth. I put down my fork into my plate of spaghetti and meatballs, and I fold my arms across my chest to emphasize the seriousness of the situation.

Adam pushes his metal-rimmed glasses up his nose and shakes his head at me across the dining table. He's really managed to perfect the disheveled scientist look over the years. Aside from the spectacles, his short, light brown hair perpetually has that "just rolled out of bed" look, no matter what the time of day is. And I've never actually managed to catch him with his shirt buttoned properly. Right now, his checkered polyester shirt is off by about two buttons. I have to sit on my hands to suppress my urge to fix it.

I'm kind of the opposite. I feel uncomfortable if I have even one strand of hair out of place. The neat cotton dress shirts and fitted skirts I wear to work are what I generally wear all the time these days. If I go more than a week without a professional manicure, I start getting antsy. I swear I haven't always been such a square.

"You saw a white rabbit outside my house …" Adam repeats, a mildly amused look in his soft brown eyes.

"With a timepiece around its neck," I add.

"And you think this is some sort of experiment I'm doing?" Now Adam is outright smirking at me.

When you say it like that, anything sounds stupid, doesn't it?

"Come on, Claudia," he says. "It probably belongs to my neighbor's kid or something. A pet rabbit."

"Yeah," I mumble, although it's really hard to push away the feeling that there was something very different about that rabbit, and that Adam isn't entirely telling the truth. But he won't 'fess up to me, and I'm beginning to sound crazy to my own ears.

Of course, it's pretty hard to sound crazy when you're dating a guy who calls himself an inventor.

I'm sure in the olden days, being an inventor was a real career. It was something you could put on your business cards. For example, Thomas Edison and Leonardo da Vinci were inventors, and nobody thought they were antisocial weirdos, as far as I can tell. But in the twenty-first century, if you go around telling people you're an inventor, people start to think you're a little off.

Not that Adam isn't a sweet guy and all. He's even invented a few things for me—he rigged up a button on my wall that I could press that would make my remote control start beeping because I complained that I was always losing it. (I called him in a panic once and made him help me comb the whole apartment until we found the remote. Do you know where it was? In the *refrigerator*. Honestly, I think sometimes I'm losing my mind.)

"So it's not some kind of computer robot rabbit?" I ask Adam, because I still just don't believe him.

He grins adorably at me. "A robot rabbit?"

I shrug. "Maybe it's for kids who want a pet but not have to feed them or clean up their crap."

"Oh, I see," Adam says, still grinning. "As a kid, you always wanted a rabbit, but you were worried it was going to crap all over the place and you'd have to clean it up."

I sense he's not taking me seriously here. "No, that's not what I'm saying."

"No, I completely get it," Adam says. "For your next birthday, you want a robot rabbit. I'm on it, Claudia. You don't need to keep hinting."

Okay, that's enough of that. I swat at him with my hand, and he grabs my wrist. Our eyes meet and I get that "butterflies in the stomach" feeling. It's almost overpowering. We've been together over a year, yet I still find Adam unbearably sexy. It's weird because Adam isn't the kind of man I would have dated in my younger years—I was so immature that I probably would have seen him at a party and made fun of him behind his back. But my concept of "sexy" has evolved considerably over time.

Smart, sweet, nice-looking, well-off guy who adores me = sexy

Devastatingly handsome starving artist who chases anyone in a skirt = unsexy

"Come here," Adam says softly as we continue to gaze into each other eyes.

I get up from my seat and settle into Adam's lap, feeling the tight muscles in his chest and arms against my body. He pulls me toward him and starts to kiss me in that gentle, tender way he always does, running his fingers through my ash blond hair. You wouldn't think it to look at him, nerdy science guy and all, but Adam is a really good kisser. Of all the men I've ever kissed, the kisses with him are the most intense, the ones that make my whole body tingle. Even more so than with Kyle, who had the tongue stud.

On a scale of one to ten, I would give Adam's kisses a nine. Maybe a nine point five on a good day.

After several minutes of making out, Adam lifts his hands off me and puts them on the wheels of his chair so he can push away from the dining table. That's another thing about Adam that's different than any other guy I've ever dated — he's disabled. And not just a little limp or something. He needs a wheelchair. All the time. He cannot walk at all.

"I'm going to make you the best robot rabbit you've ever seen," Adam whispers as his breath tickles my neck. Okay, now I'm starting to worry he's not kidding.

"I don't want a robot rabbit," I say, pulling away from him. I try to sound stern. "I mean it, Adam. Don't make me a robot rabbit."

He laughs and tugs at a lock of my hair.

"Relax, Claudia. I was just teasing you." I let out a little sigh of relief, but I shouldn't have worried. Even though he's a bit of a clueless scientist guy, he's generally surprisingly perceptive when it comes to me and what I like or want. "I've still got a few months before your birthday, and trust me, I'm going to get you something amazing."

I have absolutely no doubt in my mind that Adam will get me something amazing for my birthday. It will probably be some combination of really thoughtful and painfully expensive, if his previous gifts are any indication. Adam always gets me the best gifts.

Too bad it won't be the one thing I really want.

***

Since Adam cooked dinner, I clear the table. I take the plates and glasses, and load up the dishwasher for him. I notice one of the plates has a little chip in it and I hesitate, trying to decide whether or not to throw it out. Adam could use some new plates as of, like, five years ago, but I sense it might not be appropriate to take the initiative to buy him some. You have to be careful in a relationship about crossing certain lines.

The dishes, for example. He really didn't want me to start doing them for him—he fought me tooth and nail on that one. "They're *my* dishes, Claudia," he insisted. I pointed out that I was practically living at his house now and he was taking out the trash. So it only seemed fair that I'd pitch in and help with the chores.

I love spending time at Adam's brownstone. Despite his eccentricities, it's a very normal house, if a little messy and uninspired. His living room has a widescreen TV, a couch that's ripped and stained and far too old (like everything non-technological that Adam owns), but very comfortable, and a coffee table that's covered in rings because Adam's never heard of a coaster. The inventing is confined to one room of the house and never overflows into the main living area. Adam's study is the one room I've never yet entered.

After I get the dishwasher going, I find Adam in the living room, hunched over his desktop computer. The screen is completely filled with some coding language—just looking at it makes my head ache. When I get closer, he minimizes the window on his screen. "Hey," he says. "Thanks for getting the dishes started."

"You should be relaxing," I scold him. "You've been working way too hard lately." Of the nights I've spent here in the last two weeks, he's stayed up hours past when I went to bed.

"You know I'm a workaholic," he says, winking at me. "That's why you'd hate living with me."

I wince. This is a little game Adam has been playing very recently called You Don't Really Want to Live With Me. He takes it very seriously. It's all part of larger game called You Don't Really Want to Marry Me. I'm not very fond of this game.

Here's the deal with me and Adam: we've been dating over a year. Granted, that's not a huge amount of time. But I'm not twenty years old here. I'm thirty-six and, as he noted, I've got a birthday coming up in a few months. If I had a baby now, I'd already be advanced maternal age. And I'm not having a baby now. I'm not even married. I'm not even *engaged*.

Adam is even older than I am. He's thirty-eight. And he's not a *young* thirty-eight, either. I like to think I could pass for thirty or even younger, but Adam can't. He looks thirty-eight. Hell, he looks forty, even forty-five, easy. Not because he's fat or out of shape or balding, because he isn't any of those things. He's slim and muscular in his upper body, and he's got all his hair, but he's got almost as much gray in his hair as he's got brown, and he's got more lines on his face than he ought to, especially around his eyes. Not that it's a bad thing in terms of his looks. He's one of those guys like Sean Connery who is just going to get more attractive as he gets older. When he's seventy, he's probably going to have hot young forty-year-olds chasing him down, while I'll be a little old lady with a hump on my back.

His looks initially seemed like a sign of maturity to me, a sign that he was the sort of guy who was ready for a commitment. And we fit so well together, me and Adam. More than I thought we would when I first met him at a mutual friend's dinner party. He treated me like a queen, and I mistakenly got the idea in my head that if I brought up marriage, he'd jump at the idea (figuratively). But he didn't. He got quiet, just like every other freaking guy did. And that's why he fights me every time I want to wash a goddamn plate.

And it stinks because Adam is the first guy that I've really seen myself growing old with. I can just see us at seventy years old, me still bringing him my futuristic computer when I've got a virus and he needs to get rid of it. And then I fix the buttons on his shirt with one of my arthritic hands, and bat away the hot young forty-year-olds with the other.

"I wouldn't hate living with you," I insist, for what feels like the trillionth time. "I'm practically living here already. Why don't we make it official so I don't have to feel like a nomad?"

He raises his eyebrows at me. "You feel like a nomad?"

"I'm carrying around panties in my purse, Adam," I say. I'm half tempted to dig them out and shake them in his face. "You think I enjoy that?"

"I gave you a drawer to use," he mumbles, his eyes lowered.

Yes, he gave me a drawer. One drawer. And he lets me keep a travel bottle of shampoo and one of conditioner in his shower, because I told him his combo shampoo plus conditioner makes my hair feel like straw. And he used to let me keep a toothbrush on his sink until he insisted that I start using his electric toothbrush (with my own head), explaining it was better for my teeth.

But I don't want a freaking drawer or a toothbrush on his sink. I want a ring. Of course, I'm not going to say that to him now. We've had this conversation before and I know where it's headed, and it's not in the direction of the nearest jewelry store. There's no point in pushing him when he's clearly not ready. "I love you," I say instead. "I just want to be with you."

"I love you too, Claudia," he says. "But …"

Adam leans forward in his wheelchair, rubbing his knees, looking really uncomfortable. He told me once before the reason why he had trouble settling down, but I can't accept it. We're *right* for each other. I don't want to be one of those awful "ultimatum women" so I won't do that to him. But how long am I supposed to wait patiently for him to be ready?

"Don't be mad," Adam pleads with me.

"I'm not," I say. Well, I am. But I'm trying not to be. When I was in my twenties, I always pitied those women who made relationships all about pushing for commitment, yet here I am, close to doing it myself. It's something I vowed I'd never do. And I won't.

"Sit down on the couch," Adam says. "I'll go get you the foot massager and give you a back rub."

The foot massager. It's another thing Adam invented for me. It used to be a foot bath, but he rigged it up with mechanical brushes to give me an actual foot massage that's better than anything I've ever experienced in a spa. He made it in less than a week, after I told him how much I love foot massages. Then he rubs my neck and back when my feet sit in the bath. His hands are so strong—he gives great massages that basically drain all the tension out of my body.

I just wish I had met him before The Bitch ruined him for good.

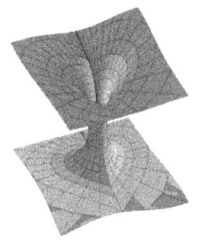

Two

This is how I found out about The Bitch:

Adam and I had been going out for about three months. We were double dating with my friend Nancy and her husband Duke, who had worked with Adam for years and also apparently played poker with him every other Friday night. We were sitting at a restaurant while Nancy fretted over the new babysitter, checking her phone every two minutes to make sure she hadn't missed an emergency call, and Duke kept telling her over and over again to calm down. At one point, Duke said to Adam, "Never have kids." Adam laughed and Duke added, "I'm telling you, you're probably lucky it took you so long to get over that girl."

Adam's eyes widened, but Duke didn't elaborate and I pretended like I didn't hear. It was still way too early in our relationship to reveal my jealous side.

But I'm only human. I couldn't help but wonder: who was "that girl"?

Over the next several months, I'd keep hearing more and more tidbits about *that girl*, and each time, I tried to ignore it. But the more I heard, the more I realized how important *that girl* was in his life. "She was all Adam could talk about for probably a year, maybe longer," his friend Drew told me. "He thought she was The One. He kept talking about inventing something for her that would convince her to come back to him, even though we kept telling him she was never coming back." I got the sense that even as recently as a couple of years ago, he'd still been talking about her.

Her name was Jessica. Actually, I'm not sure if that was her real name, but I knew this really mean girl in high school named Jessica, so that's what I've been calling her secretly in my head. Since I'll surely never meet her, for all intents and purposes, it's become her name. My Jessica had red curls, so I picture The Bitch as having long, red curls going down her back and perfect porcelain skin. In my head, she's beautiful. And in real life, I'm pretty sure she was beautiful, too.

It was Adam's older sister Kim, briefly in town from Akron, Ohio, where he grew up, who eventually spilled the dirt while the two of us were out having lunch together. It took two glasses of wine and about a dozen hints from me to get the whole story out of her.

"It was a few years after Adam got hurt," she told me. "It was his first relationship after his injury, so he was really vulnerable, you know? He thought he was in love, that he'd found the girl of his dreams. He was completely insane over her. We were all pretty skeptical, to say the least."

The girl of his dreams. Not exactly the kind of thing you want to hear about one of your boyfriend's exes. "So what happened?"

"She dumped him," Kim said. "Completely broke his heart. He was never the same after that. In a lot of ways."

"Like what?"

"He'd always been pretty practical about relationships," she said. "Very down to earth. But when it came to this girl, it was like he'd lost his freaking mind. He kept talking about how he was going to get her back, even though I told him she had no interest in coming back. It took years before he was even willing to date any other women."

Kim saw the look on my face and blanched. "I shouldn't have told you that," she said. She glanced regretfully at her wine glass. "Adam made me swear I wouldn't."

"It's okay," I said, even though I had a huge lump in my throat.

"Don't worry, Claudia," she said, patting my hand. "He's definitely over her by now. And he really likes you."

Yes, he really likes me. But he isn't "completely insane" over me. At least, I don't think he is—if he were, I assume he'd want to marry me or at least live with me. Honestly, I don't think any man has been "completely insane" over me in my entire life. I'm not even sure what that's like. Obviously, I don't have Jessica's feminine wiles.

So here I am, over ten years later, trying to compete with a girl who has become, in his mind, the ideal of perfection. I've asked him about her, and he swears it's not true, that he hates her, that she contributed to wrecking his life, but I can tell he still loves her. This Bitch broke his heart, but he's still stuck on her.

How am I supposed to compete with that?

I can't, that's how. Once a woman ruins a guy, it's pretty hard to un-ruin him. I'm beginning to worry that the only thing to do at this point is to move on because Adam will never be able to.

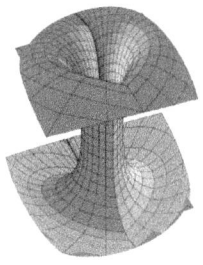

Three

Two days later, at about ten a.m., I start seeing zigzags of light in front of six-year-old Jayden McNamara's face as he struggles to read from our book about a fox and a turtle that become friends. This is the most god-awful, boring book on the planet, but unfortunately for me, I don't get to decide what my first graders get to read. Basically, the principal hands me a book about foxes and turtles and says, "This is what the children will be reading, Claudia."

"Greg was the best ..." Jayden hesitates, stuck on the next word. The word is "fox." This is a book about a fox and a turtle and the kid somehow can't read the word "fox." I think I have completely failed as a teacher. "Fff ... friend?"

"It's 'fox,' you idiot," Olivia Richards pipes up, shaking her French-braided pigtails. Now the zigzag of light is over Olivia's face.

"Olivia!" I snap. "Don't use words like that to speak to your classmates!" Even though I'd been thinking the same thing, I still have to give Olivia a time-out in the corner. First grade is so unfair.

As Jayden starts reading again, I feel the first jab of throbbing pain in my left temple. Within a minute, it feels like someone has started to play the bongo drums in the left side of my head. The lights in the room seem horribly bright. And somehow, Jayden's reading skills have deteriorated further.

"Good job," I manage to say as he finally (finally!) reaches the end of the paragraph.

I know I have to call on someone else to read now, so I pick Jack Anderson, who is a pretty good reader and will probably not need much help. Because right now, I'm in the middle of a full-on migraine attack and the thought of another kid struggling to read a three-letter word makes me want to hop out the window.

I started getting migraine headaches back in my mid-twenties. They had the usual triggers: chocolate, my period, first graders who couldn't read the word "fox." They used to be pretty intense, forcing me to call in sick more than once and hide in my dark bedroom for hours on end. A neurologist started me on a medication that helped a little but never relieved them entirely. But in the last year, since I've been with Adam, the migraines have decreased significantly in frequency, going from once a week to maybe every other month.

This is a bad one. By lunch period, I feel like I'm going to die and/or vomit. While the kids are down in the cafeteria, I go to the assistant principal Carla Prentice's office and tell her that I'm going to have to call out sick. Carla is sitting in her office, peering at her ancient desktop computer, her reading glasses riding low on her nose. She gives me a funny look. "Are you hungover, Claudia?"

"It's a migraine," I explain, unable to even muster up any indignation. If I were hungover, I definitely wouldn't have waited till lunchtime to call out.

Carla looks skeptical. Carla is one of those schoolmarm types who never got married and cares *way* too much about work. What scares me is that sometimes when I look at her, it's like I'm looking twenty years into my future. I'm definitely evolving in that direction. It freaks me out enough that I undo the top button on my white blouse.

"Fine," Carla says. "Hopefully, you'll be recovered by tomorrow."

I nod, knowing I have a surefire remedy.

I don't even bother attempting to take the

subway home because I know from experience how miserable that journey can be in the middle of a migraine attack. I hail a taxi, sucking up the twenty-dollar charge, and shut my eyes till I get back to Adam's house.

It's Thursday, which means Adam will be working from home today. Believe it or not, he doesn't earn a living through his inventing. He actually has a full-time job as a computer programmer, although he won a considerable amount of money in a lawsuit following his accident. He probably doesn't have to work, but like me, I know he enjoys his job.

When Adam opens the door to his brownstone, I can't help but get the feeling that I've interrupted something important. I've gotten this feeling before, notably when I walked in on a previous boyfriend and the woman he was cheating on me with. Yes, that really happened. But I know Adam would definitely never do that. He does sort of look like he's just been in bed, but that's Adam's usual. The only reason his shirt isn't buttoned incorrectly is that he's wearing a gray and brown T-shirt, which doesn't have buttons.

Whatever I interrupted, Adam doesn't say anything about it. When he sees me standing there, my fingers simultaneously shielding my eyes and massaging my temples, his brow creases in concern. "Migraine?" he asks.

I nod.

"Come here, you." He takes my hand and pulls me into his lap. He wheels me slowly in the direction of his bedroom, being careful about running over the imperfections in the floorboards. I was dating Adam for about a month when I was at his house and suffered my first migraine. I told him I was going to go home, but he insisted that I stay, saying he was going to take care of me. "I used to know someone who got migraines," he told me. "I'll fix you right up." He set me up in his bed, shut off all the lights in his house, and turned on music at low volume. Mozart. He transferred into bed next to me and held me tightly against his warm body.

It was amazingly effective. So every time I get a migraine these days, I don't bother with the Imitrex. I go straight to his house and he takes care of me.

I feel Adam's footplate bump gently against the side of his bed. "Time to get out," he whispers in my ear. I crawl into bed, and he goes around, shutting off all the lights. I squeeze my eyes shut, and I feel the bed move as Adam transfers in next to me. His body feels warm and safe next to mine and I feel the pain beginning to ebb. And as the pain disappears, I fall into a deep sleep.

***

After a migraine, I can sometimes sleep for, like, twenty hours straight. I guess my body expends a lot of energy creating all that pain.

After this particular migraine, I wake up at two in the morning. Adam isn't in bed next to me, which is a little odd considering the time. But I guess he could be making up for the time he lost working thanks to me. Adam is a chronic insomniac, so it's not entirely unusual for him to be awake at two a.m. if he hasn't taken a sleeping pill. And sometimes even if he *has* taken a sleeping pill.

I'm actually starving by now, because I didn't eat lunch or dinner. At least maybe I'll lose a pound or two from this. I'm on what Adam calls a "perpetual diet." I'm ten pounds overweight (okay, more like twenty if I'm being completely honest), and I'm constantly on a mission to shed them. It's just depressing to know that I'm two pants sizes larger than I was ten years ago. Unfortunately, it seems like those extra pounds have permanently fused themselves to my bones. No amount of salad or diet soda is enough to get rid of them.

Dating Adam hasn't helped the diet situation. He has a woman who does his shopping for him (and cleans, although his place always seems kind of naturally cluttered), so his fridge is usually stocked. And my boyfriend is actually a really amazing cook, especially considering most men I've dated have trouble making anything more sophisticated than TV dinners.

When Adam and I had been going out for about a month, he invited me to his house for a dinner of chicken marsala. I didn't have high hopes, so I was shocked when I took my first bite. "This is really good!" I exclaimed.

"Shocking, huh?" he said, although I could tell he was pleased.

"How'd you make it?" I asked. He'd recently told me about being an inventor, and I imagined some sort of machine that you feed raw ingredients into and it goes through a series of pulleys and frying pans and eventually spits out a full meal. I'm pretty sure every inventor I've ever seen in movies has had one of those.

"I coated the chicken in flour and salt and pepper and oregano," he explained. "And I simmered it in the frying pan in oil, butter, and marsala wine." Apparently, there were no pulleys involved. "Why? How do you make it?"

And that's when I had to confess that I am completely hopeless in the kitchen. But he took it well. "Don't worry," he said, grinning at me. "Only one of us needs to be able to cook, right?"

As I think about that night, I start actually getting a little hungry for chicken marsala, although that's probably too much to hope for.

Still, if Adam is awake, I know he'll insist on fixing me something good to eat. Rubbing my eyes, I stumble in the direction of his kitchen, but when I pass through the living room on the way to the kitchen, I notice that Adam's computer isn't on and he's not here at all. I assumed he had to be at his computer working if he was anywhere, but he's not. So where the hell is he? It's two in the morning, after all.

I hear a loud thump and lift my head. The noise came from Adam's spare room. The one where he does his inventing. The one that I've never been inside in the entire year we've been together.

Do you know the story of Bluebeard? It's a French folktale about a rich guy with a very ugly blue beard. He has this secret room that he forbids his wife to go inside, even though he gives her the key for some reason. Naturally, she goes into the room, and she finds the murdered bodies of all of Bluebeard's previous wives.

Of course, it's a little hard not to make a comparison. I mean, hello? Forbidden room? What is he *doing* in there? Chopping up the bodies of his previous wives?

Nah, that doesn't seem very likely. After all, Adam doesn't have any previous wives because he has *commitment issues*.

Still, my heart is pounding as I creep in the direction of the spare room. The door is closed but I see a light coming from underneath.

He's in there all right. But what is he doing?

There's a thumping noise, following by a loud whooshing sound. For some reason, I shiver and when I look down at my forearm, I see goose bumps standing up on my skin. Seriously, what is going on in there? I don't hear anything that sounds like he's with another woman, unless he's literally *banging* her in there. No, he's almost definitely doing some kind of work.

I see a flash of bright light under the door and I instinctively take a step back. Adam never shares with me what he's been working on in there, and I wonder if it's possible it might be something dangerous. What if he's working on something radioactive? What if he's going to set off an atomic bomb or something?

Nah, that doesn't seem too likely either.

I raise my hand, poised to knock on the door. I've never interrupted him in the middle of his work in the room. I can't imagine he'd be upset, but … maybe he would. Maybe I should just leave him be.

My hunger forgotten, I turn around and go back to bed. But this time I don't sleep quite so easily.

***

I do eventually drift off around four in the

morning, and Adam still hasn't come back to bed. But to my relief, when my phone alarm goes off at seven the next morning, he's lying next to me. He's sound asleep, blowing air softly through his parted lips, his right arm flung across his forehead. I try not to wake him, but I can't resist giving him a quick kiss. He stirs briefly, murmurs, "Love you," then gropes for me to give me a kiss of his own before he falls back asleep.

Just as I'm slipping on my shoes and getting ready to go out the door, I hear my cell phone vibrating within my purse. I check the phone and see that it's my parents calling. After a hesitation, I decide to pick up. "Hi, Mom," I say, knowing that of my parents, she's the one who always calls.

"Hello, Claudia," Mom says. She sounds so bright and chipper since she and my father permanently relocated to Florida last year, although they kept their old apartment so they can still call themselves New Yorkers. It makes me feel old to have parents who are retired and living in Florida, that's for sure. But they love it there. Dad apparently has a tan and he's taken up golfing. "Sorry to bother you in the morning …"

"That's all right," I say. She often calls in the morning, because she wakes up at six a.m. every morning for some reason now that she lives in Florida. Her entire sleeping schedule has shifted—she and Dad never go to bed any later than nine o'clock.

"I called your cell last night, and you didn't answer, so I called Adam. He said you had a migraine." My mother tends to freak out when she can't reach me, so I gave her Adam's cell number for emergencies. She tends to overestimate what an emergency is and call him far too often, but he doesn't seem to mind.

"The migraine is better."

"Glad to hear it, honey," Mom says. "And how's Adam? He sounded tired."

My parents shocked me by really loving Adam. When I first told my mother I was dating a guy with a disability, she sounded mildly disapproving, so I was definitely worried when we all got together for dinner several months ago. I put it off forever, making up excuses about how Adam had to work or the weather in New York was too crummy. Adam seemed to realize I was avoiding the meeting, and he finally said to me, "Calm down, Claudia. Parents love me."

It turned out he was right. I thought for sure they'd be angry that I was dating a guy who was disabled, but they really took to him. I think they liked the fact that he's a little older and more serious than other men I've dated. And they could tell how good he was to me.

"He's fine," I say. "Working hard, that's all."

Mom lowers her voice. "Any ring, yet?"

Does my mother want her daughter to be married, like, yesterday? Why yes, she does. And I made the horrible mistake of mentioning to her that I thought he might ask me — that was before Adam's admission of his commitment issues. Now I'll never hear the end of it.

"Not yet, Mom," I say. "Look, we've only been together a year. It's still early …"

"You're thirty-six, Claudia!" Mom says. "Don't you want to have children? Listen, you have to push him a little. He's so crazy about you. I'm sure he'll ask you if you give him a little nudge …"

Don't count on it. "Mom, I have to go to work …"

"Oh, wait, let me put Daddy on!"

I listen to the shuffling on the other end of the line and finally my father picks up. For about thirty years, my father was a high-powered malpractice attorney in Manhattan. If you wanted to skewer some doctor, you called Don Williams. Until 2009 when he had a stroke.

It could have been worse. The stroke left him with slightly garbled speech that Mom and I have learned to understand pretty well by now, a face that droops a bit on the right, and a right hand that doesn't work very well. Also, he needs a cane when he walks outside of the house. The big thing was that the stroke forced him to retire from his practice and start taking it easy. In that sense, it's been a good thing, but I still wish it didn't have to happen that way.

As a kid, I always thought of my father as being Superman. He was big, strong, and nothing could hurt him. Even as an adult, I mostly thought of him that way. Then when I saw him lying in bed after his stroke, he seemed so feeble. And old. In the few months after the stroke, his graying hair turned completely white. It made me realize for the first that I wasn't going to have my father around forever.

"Hi, Claudia," Dad says into the phone, speaking slowly to enunciate his words like the speech therapist taught him. "How are you?"

"I'm fine," I say, grateful that he at least won't be probing into my personal life.

"How's Adam?" he asks. Dad loves Adam. Partially because being with Adam makes him feel better about the fact that he needs a cane to walk. But also because Adam fixed his laptop for him.

"Adam's fine," I say.

"Please marry him so your mother shuts up about it," Dad says.

I laugh. I figure worrying about me getting married and having kids gives my mother something to do. Once I check those items off my list, what will she have to nag me about? Her life will probably seem quite empty. Well, except for the grandkids.

In any case, it doesn't sound like it's something I'll have to worry about any time soon.

***

Our first anniversary, one month ago, was when things between me and Adam started to go downhill.

Adam took me to this really nice French restaurant because he knows I find French food romantic. I don't know why that is exactly, but I just do. I mean, if someone told you they were ordering rooster, you'd probably make a face, but if they said they were eating *coq au vin*, you'd say that sounded delicious.

I could tell Adam was going out of his way to make the night special. Instead of the usual single rose he brings for me, he had a dozen delivered to my door that morning. And he pre-ordered a bottle of really good wine to make sure it would be available for us. It was incredibly expensive but definitely not out of his price range. And Adam himself looked so sexy. He actually made an effort to button his dark blue shirt with all the right buttons and tamed his hair at least a little. And he wore a tie.

He got us a secluded table for two in the back of the restaurant. The lighting was dim and there was a single candle between us. As we waited for our wine to arrive, Adam took my hand and said to me, "I love you so much, Claudia. You're the best thing in my whole goddamn life."

So really, you can't blame a girl for getting the wrong idea.

Yes, I thought he was going to propose. I was absolutely *sure* he was going to propose. I was so sure that I was swishing my wine around in the glass, making sure I wasn't missing seeing a diamond ring, scared I had swallowed it. I dug through my chocolate mousse with my fork, searching for it. But it wasn't there.

And then the waiter pulled away our dessert plates and the opportunity to hide the ring in food was lost. Still, I was hopeful. And then Adam pulled out a blue velvet box and I nearly fainted. Before he could even open it, I started tearing up, murmuring, "Yes, yes, yes …"

Except Adam didn't ask me to marry him. He just looked confused.

The box contained earrings, by the way. Diamond earrings that were beautiful and horribly expensive, and I absolutely hated them. I wanted to take them and throw them in Adam's face.

"I'm sorry," he said, a deep crease between his brows. "Did you think I was going to …? I mean, I didn't know you were expecting …"

"How could you not know?" I asked him, trying to keep my voice down so as not to let on how very upset I was. I mean, he did get me some beautiful and expensive earrings. I should have been grateful.

"Well, it's only been a year," he pointed out.

"*Only a year*," I repeated. "Adam, we're not *kids*. How long exactly are we supposed to wait here?"

Adam tugged at his tie, loosening the knot like he needed some extra air. I'd seen men look that way before. It made my stomach turn. "I don't know ..."

"Didn't you just say that I'm the best goddamn thing in your whole life?"

"Yeah," he admitted. "So ... why do we have to spoil it?"

"Spoil it?" My voice rose an octave, and I cleared my throat quickly. As much as I didn't want to turn into the kind of woman I'd always felt sorry for, I also needed to be straight with him: "Adam, that's bullshit and you know it."

He slumped down in his wheelchair, his expression glassy. I think it was safe to say all the romance had been sucked out of the evening. "I'm just not ready yet, Claudia."

I really loved him, but I hated him for saying that. I hated him for being like every other guy, especially when I loved him so much more than I loved any other guy and I thought he felt the same way.

Something changed between us that night. I felt like I'd suddenly evolved into this nagging girlfriend that I really didn't want to be. I knew that our relationship had to move forward or it would die, but it wasn't up to me. I hinted at marriage a few more times or even me moving in with him, but he always had an excuse. Something about not being ready, or that I deserved better than him, or my personal favorite: that The Bitch had messed him up so badly that he just couldn't settle down.

Part of me kind of feels for him. I mean, he had this awful experience with another woman, and it can be hard to bounce back from that. But there are other fish in the sea, Adam. It's pretty sad if you can't get over some girl from ten years ago.

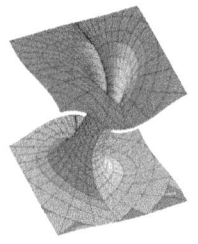

Four

I have a spectacularly bad day at work that makes me glad my migraine is completely gone. The student bathroom is just across the hall from my classroom, so when one of my kids raises a little hand and says, "Miss Williams, I gotta use the bathroom," I give them a pass and they scoot across the hall to use the bathroom then come on back like a good little girl or boy.

Except today Sophia Wright decides that after using the bathroom, she wants to take a little stroll around the school. After she doesn't return for fifteen minutes, I finally have to contact the principal's office, and we locate her finger-painting in the empty art classroom. I think her parents may have forgotten to administer her ADHD meds this morning.

This incident drags me into a meeting after school, where we have to discuss how to fix things so that we don't have "a repeat of Sophia Wright." Considering she was never in any real danger, I feel that punishing Sophia would be sufficient, but I'm in the minority. Ideas that get tossed around include forcing every kid to have a bathroom buddy (but then we'd lose two of them!) and having designated "bathroom time" where I stand there and watch every kid in my class pee, and the kids can't go any other time (great idea, as long as they're wearing diapers — six year olds are not skilled at "holding it in").

Halfway through the meeting, I get a text from Adam, which I check surreptitiously under the table: *You coming over tonight?*

I think of last night and feel relieved he isn't being weird today: *Sure.*

His reply comes back quickly: *Need to show you something. Important.*

What is it?

Can't say. Just come. Love you.

One thing I have to say for Adam, he certainly knows how to intrigue a girl.

I go back to my apartment in Chelsea after work to shower and grab some new clothes. My apartment is a tiny studio, which is honestly the best I can afford on my salary — it's a crime how underpaid elementary school teachers are. I've put up a lot of mirrors to make it look bigger, but it's really small. All I've got room for is a sofa bed, a tiny wooden desk, and a bookcase.

I've checked my finances and I think I may have enough to upgrade to a one-bedroom apartment, where I'll have room for an actual sofa *and* a bed, but I've been holding off. I haven't given up hope Adam will ask me to move in with him. I think I can persuade him — I just haven't figured out how.

But for now, I'm stuffing a blouse and underwear into my purse for tomorrow. One drawer just isn't enough.

I can't help but wonder about Adam's weird disappearance last night. He's never done anything like that before, as far as I can remember. I'm actually starting to really wonder what's so important that Adam wants to show me.

Chances are, it's not an engagement ring.

If I had to guess, based on last night, I'd imagine it's an invention. Adam shows me nearly all his inventions these days, and I have to say, it's adorable how excited he gets over them. He's made several things that are specifically for me, and he's so proud of himself when he shows them to me. I feel like it's sort of romantic to think of him slaving over some invention just to make me happy.

Adam waited until date number five to drop the inventor bomb on me. I guess he figured I'd think it was too weird and go running for the hills, which wasn't entirely inaccurate. At least he has good insight into how weird it is.

The way he told me was that he brought me a single red rose. He'd given me roses before, but this time when I brought the rose close to my face to inhale its scent, it started playing Peter Frampton's "Baby I Love Your Way." That's one of my favorite songs, a fact I didn't even remember having shared with him. He must have asked my friends what songs I liked.

"There's a metal chip that senses the heat of your face and plays music," Adam informed me, somewhat shyly.

I looked at the rose in amazement. "Where did you get it?"

"I made it," he said, as if anything else would have been ridiculous. Then he added, "For you."

"You made it yourself?" I asked, still incredulous. I twirled the rose between my thumb and index finger. "Like, from scratch?"

"Well, I didn't mine the metal from the earth myself," he said. "But yeah, sort of from scratch. I like doing that kind of thing. Inventing new stuff."

"Wow," I said.

"Hmm," Adam said. "When you say 'wow,' does that mean 'wow' as in 'my boyfriend is too incredible for words' or 'wow' as in 'I had no idea my boyfriend was such a loser geek'?"

"The first one," I told him, smelling the rose again as Peter Frampton's music filled my ears. It smelled good *and* it played music. Truth be told, I fell a little bit in love at that moment. I mean, my boyfriend invented something for me. How cool is that?

Most of Adam's inventions are minor, little devices he rigs up. He's never invented anything before that he described as "important." It makes me wonder if he really does have something special planned for this evening. Maybe he isn't going to ask me to marry him, but at least maybe he really does want us to move in together. That would be great.

I consider dressing up, going so far as to pull out my dark green Versace dress that I know is Adam's favorite, but I ultimately opt for my usual jeans and a sweater. He'll be dressed casually, so I'll feel silly all dressed up. Plus it's painfully obvious that Adam couldn't really care less what I wear. He is less concerned with fashion than anyone I've ever met.

I brave the subway and make it uptown in about half an hour. It's quiet on his street, and I can hear the clip-clop of my sandals echoing against the pavement. Adam lives in a largely residential area, but just a few blocks away, there are tons of restaurants, including a dim sum place that's to die for. One thing I *don't* see today are any rabbits. Not even one. Thank God.

When Adam opens the door to his house, he's smiling and his face has a glow that's very familiar. I squint at him, "Have you been drinking?"

Adam smiles wider and shows me his thumb and forefinger about an inch apart. "Just a bit. It's a really exciting day. *Really* exciting."

I slip inside and close the door behind me. "Is that so?"

"Life changing," he says, his brown eyes wide behind his spectacles.

"Is that so?" I ask again, my heart pounding slightly. Life changing? What does that mean?

Adam nods. "Definitely."

He wheels himself down the hallway and into the living room and I follow him, my heart still thumping in my chest. I really have no idea what he's going to show me, but I'm starting to get the feeling it's nothing romantic. I mean, if it were, he'd have me in his lap right now. I wouldn't be racing after him, trying to keep up because he's so damn excited.

When we get into the living room, Adam points proudly to something in the middle of the room. "Here it is."

My jaw falls open. I know exactly what that is.

"You stole my step," I say angrily.

Adam stares at me blankly. "What?"

"My step!" I say. I cannot believe this, honestly. "You took it! I've been looking for it for months!"

Adam looks down at the step that I bought about a year ago for my step aerobics. When I started spending more time here, I brought the step over, thinking I could do my exercise DVD. I didn't even have a chance to do the video once, because when I returned to his house a few days later, the step had vanished. It's not exactly small—about two feet in length—so I genuinely couldn't understand how it had disappeared. I even asked Adam about it, and he had no clue what I was talking about.

Now it all makes sense. Adam took it. For reasons that are beyond me.

"I didn't know it was yours," he says, sounding a little baffled.

"Where did you get it?" I ask.

He shifts in his wheelchair. "I found it. In my living room."

"And you didn't think it was odd that this big step suddenly appeared in your living room one day?"

"I guess not." Adam shrugs sheepishly. The crazy thing is, I believe him. I don't think he meant to steal my step and drive me insane searching for it. He just saw it, figured it was something he needed, and took it. Remind me not to leave my wallet lying around.

"I'm sorry, Claudia," Adam says to me. "I didn't know it was yours. I can buy you a new one."

"I already bought a new one," I say. "And believe me, I will never *ever* bring it here."

"You can if you want," he says.

"No way," I say. "Obviously, my steps aren't safe around you. Whatever you made with my first step, I'm sure a second step would make it twice as good."

"I'm really sorry." Adam's cheeks are pink now. "How much was it? I'll pay you back."

I wave my hand. Adam is very generous about money, mostly because he has lots of it. He's never even close to allowed me to contribute to paying for a meal. I feel like it would be pretty insulting to make him get out his wallet and hand me bills. "It's okay."

"So, um," he says. "Can I show you what it is?"

Aside from being for step aerobics? I look closer and see that he's rigged it up to a large metal canister that's making an ominous whirring noise, as well as a small laptop computer. There are about a dozen copper wires connecting everything, and for a second, I see one of them emit a small spark. I can't even imagine what this is. I take a stab in the dark: "Is it some kind of virtual reality thing?"

Adam shakes his head. "Nope. It's a device to create wormholes in space."

I take a few steps back, horrified. "Adam, is that thing filled with *worms*? Because if it is—"

He laughs. "No, a *wormhole*. Don't you know what that is?"

At least I can say he respects me enough to assume I know as much physics as he does. "Sorry, no."

"Okay …" Adam thinks for a second. I know it's important to him that I understand this, so I try my best to focus on what he's about to say. "So pretend spacetime is a two-dimensional surface …" Aaaand he's already lost me. "If you fold this surface along a third dimension, you would create a wormhole 'bridge.' It's basically like a tunnel through different points in spacetime."

I just look at him blankly.

"You can travel through time," he finally says.

I stare at him. I must be hearing wrong. "You made a *time machine*?" I say, incredulous. "Out of my step from step aerobics?"

"It's not a time machine," Adam says, sounding a little miffed at the comparison. "It creates wormholes."

"But the purpose is to travel through time, right?"

"Yes ..."

I fold my arms across my chest. "So how is that not a time machine?"

Because he doesn't want it to be, seems to be the only answer he can come up with. Because time machines are stupid and/or fictional, and what he created is something real. But from what he's telling me, that's exactly what this is. And naturally, I'm just a bit skeptical.

"Can I show you how it works?" he asks, all full of wide-eyed eagerness.

I have to admit, I'm curious. So I follow him as he wheels over to the side of the room, where there's a rectangular object covered by a light sheet. He pulls off the sheet and underneath is a metal cage. And inside the metal cage is ...

"The rabbit!" I almost scream. It's the rabbit from the other day! I'm sure of it because it even has that black patch on its backside. And now I can hear that ticking noise again, coming from the timepiece around its neck.

"It *was* your rabbit!" I cry, now nearly furious with him. "You lied to me!"

Adam digs into his pocket and pulls out a crumpled scrap of paper. He hands it to me and I see it's a receipt. "I bought this rabbit two hours ago," he explains.

I look down at the receipt, and sure enough, it's dated with today's date. But that's obviously got to be a forgery.

Of course, Adam has never lied to me before. Not that I know of.

He bends over, opens the cage, and pulls out the rabbit. The rabbit huddles on his lap, obviously already afraid of me. Adam strokes its white fur gently. He's actually pretty great with animals, unlike me. "Now all we need is a version of this little guy that doesn't need to eat or take a crap," he says in a teasing voice.

"Shut up," I say, unable to take my eyes off the rabbit.

"His name is Albert," Adam says as the rabbit nibbles on his fingers.

"Like Albert Einstein?" I ask.

Adam looks at me blankly. "No, I just always liked the name Albert."

He wheels over to the step while Albert sits peacefully on his lap. Adam points to the laptop and shows me the screen. "We just have to adjust the settings," Adam explains. I peer at the screen, watching carefully. "So, you saw him three days ago, at seven p.m. So we just type in the date we want to go back, the time, and the amount of time that he'll be gone for … say, ten minutes. I don't want the little guy to get hurt or scared being gone too long."

"What happens when the time is up?" I'm not even sure if I'm humoring him anymore. Does this thing really work? Seriously?

"The wormhole will shrink and suck him back to his previous time," Adam says. He smiles at my horrified expression. "It won't *hurt* him or anything."

I watch as Adam carefully lays little Albert down on the step. Albert looks mildly nervous as the clock around his neck ticks loudly. Adam points out the time on the clock is accurate: seven fifteen p.m. I inch backwards, suddenly a little worried. "Have you done this before?" I ask.

"Yeah," Adam says. "With, like, objects. This is my first live trial. But I already know it's going to work."

"How do you know that?"

Adam gives me a funny look. "Because you saw Albert outside the building three days ago."

That makes some sort of crazy sense. Although I still back up a few feet before Adam clicks on a button on the computer screen that says ENTER WORMHOLE.

The entire room gets very cold all of a sudden. Frigid, like every molecule of warmth has been sucked into the wormhole. There's a flash of almost blinding light that comes from my step, and there's a loud whooshing sound, almost like a giant toilet being flushed. I'm suddenly really scared for Albert, that he's being flushed down some kind of cosmic toilet. I mean, I know he's just a rabbit, but I'd still feel really bad about it.

And then, when the light disappears and the room gets quiet again, Albert is gone.

"Where is he?" I ask, hugging my arms to my chest. It's still freezing in here and I'm covered in goose bumps.

"You mean, *when* is he?" Adam corrects me.

"Oh, my God, shut up!" I say. I know he thinks he's being cute, but seriously, this is freaky. Either he just sent a rabbit into the past or he liquidated a rabbit. Either way, it's very freaky. "When will he come back?"

Adam glances at his watch. "Oh, around now."

I'm still seeing flashes of green dancing before my eyes from when Albert disappeared. I blink a few times and rub my eyes. I wish Adam had told me to look away. Not that I would have been able to.

Just as the spots are fading a bit, another flash of light comes from the step. I quickly shield my eyes, shivering as the temperature of the room drops at least another twenty degrees. I finally drop my hand and, sitting on the steps like he never left, is Albert. I just stare at him in disbelief.

"Check out the clock," Adam says as he wheels over to the rabbit. He picks him up and I can't help but notice that Albert leaves behind two muddy footprints and a blade of grass. "Look! It's ten minutes fast!"

I stare down at the timepiece around Albert's neck. Sure enough, it says seven twenty-five p.m.

Holy shit. My boyfriend just invented a freaking time machine.

Five

Adam cracks open an expensive bottle of Chardonnay that he's been saving for a special occasion. You don't get much more special than this, I think. He's invented something that will change the course of history. Adam is going to be famous, even more so than his rabbit's namesake. Everyone in the world will know the name Adam Schaffer.

Adam still has the rabbit on his lap as I pour the wine into glasses at his dining table. "I should really do some tests on him," he says, sounding a little worried. "Make sure he's okay."

"Come on, he's fine," I say, handing Adam a glass of wine. I guess it's possible he has some horrible internal damage, but he looks pretty good. For a rabbit. I'm not sure what rabbits are supposed to be doing, but whatever it is, he's doing it. I'm pretty sure.

"He looks good," Adam admits. He takes a sip of wine, then a second, then tilts back his head and drains the whole glass. He puts down the empty cup on the dining table and rubs his eyes behind his glasses. "I can't believe … after all this time … it *worked* …"

I sit down across from him. "So what are you going to do? I mean, who do you tell about something like this?"

Adam looks down at the rabbit and strokes his fur. In the entire year I've known him, he's always had circles under his eyes. He always looks a little bit exhausted. And right now, he looks *really* exhausted and his hair is sticking up at odd angles, even more so than usual. I wonder if he spent the whole night awake, working on the machine. "Nobody," he finally says.

Nobody? What?

"What are you talking about, Adam?" I say. "An invention like this—"

"Is incredibly dangerous," he interrupts me. "You think the atomic bomb was dangerous? This is about a hundred times worse. Imagine being able to go back in time and alter history. Do you realize how awful that could be?"

"Awful?" I shake my head. "It could be

wonderful. I mean, you could go back in time and … and kill Hitler before he rose to power." I never understood before why every single time travel theoretical seems to involve killing Hitler. And now here I am, doing it myself. Oh, well.

"Right, that would be great," Adam says. "Except someone could also use the time machine to go back in time and *help* Hitler. Make him win."

Fine. It's pretty clear that if a time machine came into existence, Hitler's life would either get better or worse, but definitely not stay the same. And I can see his point, I guess. A time machine could be really dangerous in the wrong hands. But that still leaves one really important question. "So why the hell did you make it?" I ask him.

Adam just looks at me for a minute, and I think he knows the exact reason why he invented it, but he doesn't want to tell me. Instead, he grabs the bottle of wine and pours himself another glass. He doesn't drink it right away though. He swishes it around, staring at the translucent liquid. "Claudia," he murmurs.

He puts down the glass and starts pulling on his earlobe, which I've noticed he always does when he's nervous. And right now, he's getting *me* nervous. Whatever he's going to say to me, it's big. And it's not a marriage proposal either.

"I need you to go through the wormhole," he says to me in a low voice. "And I need you to stop me from getting hit by that car."

When we were dating about a month, Adam told me the story of how he was injured. He was innocently riding his bike on his way to work when he was twenty-two years old, and a taxi slammed into him, breaking his back and severing his spinal cord. He successfully sued the taxi company and received a considerable settlement, enough to finance his expensive brownstone and his inventing hobby.

I finally get it. Adam doesn't want to revolutionize the world, become famous, or even kill Hitler. He built a time machine so he'd be able to walk again.

And all I know is I don't want to do this. I love him, but I don't want to do this. I really, really don't. And he can look at me and pretty much know it.

He drops his face into his hands. "I'm sorry, Claudia," he says. "I hate myself for asking you. If there were any other way ..."

"Why can't *you* go?" I say. As I reach for my glass of wine and notice my hand won't stop shaking. A drop of wine splashes over the edge and rolls down the back of my hand.

"I wish I could," he says. "I've put metal through the machine and it doesn't do so great. My wheelchair ... probably wouldn't make it. And then I'd be screwed."

"Great," I say. "You've got a machine that apparently destroys metal and you have absolutely no issue with putting your girlfriend through it. Wonderful."

Adam lifts his brown eyes to meet mine. He has so many lines around them for someone his age—it makes me ache sometimes. "Think about it, Claudia," he says. "If I'd never broken my back, my life would have been so much easier."

So here's the crazy thing: Adam never struck me as particularly bitter about being in a wheelchair. Yes, he's had it rough. But at the same time, he's never once expressed any sort of sentiment that made me think he truly wished he could walk again. He actually seemed pretty okay with it. In fact, that accident is what made him enough money to be able to live the kind of lifestyle he wanted. But obviously I had him all wrong.

"And if I never get hurt," Adam goes on. "I'll never meet *her*."

I know who he means, of course. Her. The Bitch.

Well, he's managed to tempt me, that's for sure. After all, if Adam never meets The Bitch, then he won't be so anxious about commitment, and maybe we actually have a chance to spend the rest of our lives together. And all I have to do is risk my life being zapped through a wormhole in space. No big deal.

I wish I were a risk-taker but I'm really not. I'm terrified of taking risks. I've never gone bungee jumping or even skiing. I don't gamble when I go to casinos. I even get a little nervous about those scratch-off lottery tickets. And of all the things I could risk, I'd say my *life* is way up there.

When I don't say anything, Adam looks away. "I shouldn't have asked," he says. "I'm sorry. Forget I said anything."

"Okay, let's just forget about it," I say.

But how could I forget? Adam just offered me an opportunity to fix everything wrong with his life. And I said no.

***

The rest of the evening is pretty subdued.

I mean, my boyfriend just showed me a time machine, zapped a rabbit back in time three days, then asked me to go back in time and keep him from getting hit by a car ... and I said no. So, since all those topics are kind of off limits right now, I don't know what we can possibly talk about. The weather? The latest contestants on *American Idol*? It all seems a bit weak.

Adam asks me if I'll spend the night, and I say yes because I've got to say yes to something tonight. He hits the shower while I lie in bed in an oversized T-shirt I borrowed (i.e. stole) from him, and I play a mindless game on my phone. Adam's a night showerer, while I'm a morning showerer, which works well for our relationship because we're never both trying to hit the showers at the same time. It's also good because he's definitely not fast in the shower — it's hard to be when you can't stand up. He's got a bench in there that he transfers onto, and a second nozzle he uses that's within easy reach.

When Adam comes out of the bathroom in boxers and an undershirt, he's got a towel draped over his wheelchair, under his legs, to keep the cushion dry. The shirt is sticking to his chest a little bit from moisture, and I can make out all the muscles below the fabric. For a geeky scientist, Adam has an incredibly muscular upper body — he explained to me that it's from years of wheeling himself around full time, and I love the rock-hard pecs, delts, and biceps. His hair is still dripping wet, so that it's harder to see the gray. He looks incredibly sexy right now. But somehow, I can't help but wonder how he looked when he was twenty-two, on that day he went out with his bicycle.

"I'm sorry, Claudia," he says for what feels like the millionth time tonight.

"You don't have to apologize," I say, mostly because every time he says he's sorry, I feel a little bit worse.

"It was an asshole thing to ask you to do

that," he says.

"Yeah," I say, trying to force a smile. "You're a huge asshole." Not really. He's actually the nicest guy I've ever known.

He transfers into bed next to me and I cuddle up to his chest, while he puts his strong arm around my shoulders and hugs me close to him. I can hear the slow beat of his heart thudding in my ear. It feels so *right*, lying here with him.

"This last year with you has been perfect," Adam says, as if reading my mind.

"Yeah," I say, squeezing his chest. "It has."

"I just ..." He sighs. "I wish my life before meeting you had been different."

I press my face into his firm chest. Gradually, I hear his breathing start to slow and deepen. I'd wonder how he could sleep after a day like today, but I bet a million dollars that he swallowed a sleeping pill. I, on the other hand, am drug-free and I'm not finding sleep nearly as easy.

Eventually, I just give up that sleep is ever going to happen and wander out into the living room. I flick on the lights, although I know the layout of the house so well that I could navigate it practically in my sleep. Even the first time I walked in here, I felt *comfortable* here, like it was a place I was meant to be. Everything about Adam just always felt so right. Up until recently, when everything has felt wrong.

In the corner of the room is a large translucent red jar. It was Adam's Valentine's Day present to me, a couple of months before our failed anniversary dinner. We decided to leave it here, since it's pretty heavy and I'm here most of the time anyway. The jar is filled with gourmet jelly beans—one of my favorite treats. Under the red glass, I can make out dozens of colors representing different flavors of jelly beans.

"But how do you get them out?" I asked him when he presented it to me. The top of the jar was sealed and there was only a little rectangular metal door at the bottom, like the opening for change on an old payphone. I stuck my fingers in the door but found nothing.

"I installed an app on your phone," he explained.

I took out my phone and he showed me an icon titled "Jelly beans." I clicked on it and there was a list of dozens of jelly bean flavors. I selected "marshmallow," and a second later, I heard a clanging noise from the giant jar.

"Okay, now you can check," he told me.

Sure enough, when I stuck my finger in the rectangular door, a marshmallow-flavored jelly bean was waiting for me. I stared at it in amazement before popping it in my mouth. "How did you do that?"

He shrugged sheepishly and then launched into some detailed explanation that went right over my head. I requested a cherry-flavored jelly bean, followed by a buttered popcorn one. "It must have taken you forever to do this," I said.

"Nah," Adam said. "Maybe, like, fifty hours?"

Fifty hours. The guy works full time and still spent fifty hours slaving away to make me a present that was really cool, something he thought I'd love. Most of the guys I'd dated could hardly be bothered to pick up a box of chocolates or something. I imagined him in his lab, daydreaming about my face when I saw what he made for me. It was just about the most romantic thing I could imagine.

"Adam …" I said, my eyes filling with tears.

"Do you like it?" he asked anxiously.

"I love it," I whispered.

He dug out something concealed behind his thigh. I was a velvet rectangular box. "Because I also got you this."

The second present was a beautiful white gold necklace with a diamond heart pendant. It looked like it cost thousands of dollars. I nearly fainted when I saw it. "Adam," I said, holding it up. "This … this is all too much. I love you. You don't have to …"

"I love you too," he said quickly. "I just

want to make sure you know how much."

I put on the necklace for him, and we spent the rest of the night eating jelly beans until our stomachs ached. In my whole life, no man has ever made me feel as special and loved as Adam does. And the frustrating part is that I feel like I can never quite reciprocate. Yes, I love him, but I can't compete with these big romantic gestures. Like, for example, for that Valentine's Day, I bought Adam a *tie*. Yes, it was a really nice, expensive tie. But it was just a tie. It wasn't, like, a machine that made ties then sorted them by color or some crazy thing like that. I spent less than an hour picking it out, not fifty hours slaving away in a lab.

Sometimes I'd wrack my brain, trying to think of something I could do for Adam to let him know how deeply I cared about him. But I just couldn't think of anything as great as the things he did for me.

And now, of course, he's offering me an opportunity to make a grand romantic gesture for him. The more I think about it, the harder it is to say no.

***

Due to my insomnia the night before, I oversleep a bit the next morning. When I wake up, Adam isn't next to me in bed. As I sit up and yawn, he wheels into the room with a plate on his lap, which contains an omelet and crisp buttered toast. It smells incredible.

"I brought you breakfast in bed," he says with a crooked smile. "To make up for being a jerk last night."

"You weren't a jerk," I say as I take the plate from him and put it on my lap.

"I was," he insists. "I just wanted to try to make it up to you. I love you, Claudia."

I watch him as he transfers to get back into bed next to me. I can't help but notice the way he winces and then grabs his left shoulder as he settles into bed. "What's wrong?" I ask.

"Just my stupid shoulders." He shrugs. "They're acting up a little more than usual today."

I swallow a small bite of toast. Adam's mentioned his shoulders before. Aside from his sleeping pill, he takes a prescription painkiller for the aches associated with being in a wheelchair for sixteen years. I think of him being in pain this morning yet still going to the kitchen to make me breakfast.

I push the eggs around my plate, my appetite suddenly gone. "Adam ..." I say.

"Did I overcook them?" he asks, concerned.

"No," I say. "They're perfect."

I know I said before I don't usually take risks. But sometimes, if you want something bad enough, it might be worth it.

"All right," I say. "I'll do it."

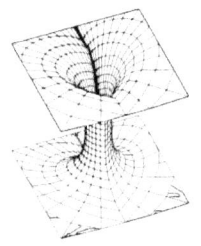

Six

Adam just stares at me, a smile spreading across his face. "You will? Really?"

It's hard to swallow because of a big lump in my throat. "Yeah, I will. I'll do it."

"Are you sure?"

Now it's my turn to stare at him. "Seriously? You just begged me to do it yesterday and now you're asking if I'm sure?" I heave a sigh. "I'm sure. As long as you're sure it's safe." Even though there's really no way he can guarantee anything like that, and I know it as well as anyone.

"It's safe," he says, with more assurance than I'd expect, considering we've had only one test subject so far. And that subject wasn't even human. "Albert is doing great. I just checked on him. His insides aren't scrambled or anything like that."

His insides aren't scrambled. Fantastic. "You're not exactly instilling me with confidence right now."

"Sorry." He seems unable to keep the huge grin off his face though. "I'm just really happy you're doing this, that's all." He adds: "I knew you would."

He did? Because I sure as hell didn't see this coming.

Adam tugs the plate of eggs and toast off my lap and puts it on the night table. And then he starts kissing me in a way that he hasn't kissed me since that anniversary dinner that I completely screwed up. He whispers that he loves me into my hair and I whisper that I love him back. "I'm going to show you how much I love you, Claudia," he breathes.

I feel his kisses going down my belly and I know what's coming. He quickly moves back into his wheelchair because that's the easiest position for him, and I feel him sliding my panties off. I have dated many men in my life, and not all of them are willing to go down on a woman (all of them are quite willing to be on the receiving end, though), but Adam is by far the best. If it were the Olympics, he'd have won a gold for the US. If he were looking for a job, he ought to put it in his resume. He's seriously that good. I'd always been kind of lukewarm on the idea of getting eaten out, mostly because a lot of guys don't really enjoy doing it and make it seem like a total chore, but let me tell you, this boy knows what he's doing. I had no clue it could be that good. We do have regular sex, but that takes a little more planning and he has less control due to his injury. Going down on me is definitely his go-to when he wants to pleasure me.

"Where did you learn how to do that?" I asked him the first time he did it for me, as he climbed back into bed next to my trembling body. I was almost levitating for a minute there.

"Why? Did you like it?" Adam asked, blinking innocently. He was totally full of shit, though. He knows he's great at it. And even if he didn't, I think my screams might have tipped him off.

"It's a little scary how good that was," I said to him. "Really, how did you get that good?"

"I took a few night courses," he said thoughtfully. "I considered getting my master's, but I would have had to take some Spanish if I did that."

I smacked him in the arm, accepting that he wasn't going to tell me any more and it was probably better that I didn't know. After all, what if he perfected his methods on The Bitch? That was definitely information I didn't need to have.

I don't know exactly why, but today is the best it's ever been. Let me just say that it's a damn good thing Mrs. Klein right above us is half deaf because I can't keep my voice down. When he finishes, I'm covered in sweat, and Adam crawls back into bed with me, kissing me and telling me over and over again how much he loves me.

***

Since Adam's eggs end up going cold, he suggests going out to brunch at one of our favorite Greek diners. Admittedly, it's nothing amazing, but somehow it just feels special. He's so happy with me right now. Every time we stop to wait for a light to change on the street, he holds my hand and sometimes pulls me down for a kiss.

The entrance to Cosmo's has a single step, which is no problem for Adam to do a wheelie over in his chair. He hops it easily and as I watch him, I can't help but comment, "By tonight, you won't need to do that anymore."

He looks up at me with this expression that seems very ... sad. Which is odd, because why would he be sad? He should be happy. By tonight, he could be walking again. He should be thrilled.

Cosmo's is one of those Greek diners that

are ubiquitous in the city. The owner Pete is a big boisterous man in his sixties who, Adam confided in me, has tried to set him up with some of his pretty Greek nieces. Pete insists on greeting all customers at the door and he reserves an extra-wide smile when he sees us enter. "Adam and Claudia!" he booms. "My favorite customers!" (I'm pretty sure he says that to everyone.)

"Hey, Pete," Adam says, and his good mood seems to have returned. He grins at Pete and he almost looks ten years younger.

"I give you the best table," Pete tells us, as he leads us to a table near the entrance. He knows we prefer to sit near the door so that Adam doesn't have to navigate between stray chairs, although he can generally do that fairly easily. He slides his wheelchair neatly underneath the red-and-white-checked tablecloth, and waves off Pete's offer of the menus. We don't need the menu at this point. I get my pancakes and Adam gets his French toast.

"So how is this going to work?" I ask him, after we've placed our orders with our waiter, Pete's nephew Nico.

Adam runs his hand through his graying hair. "You're sure you want to do this?"

"Adam!" Is he hoping I'll change my mind? Seriously.

"Okay, fine." He nods. "All right, this is what you're going to do ..." He pauses to chew on his lip. "My bicycle got hit by the taxi on September 23, 1997, at roughly eight forty-five a.m. Sixteen years ago. I left my apartment building at eight in the morning."

"So I guess you can send me back at like... seven thirty?"

Adam shakes his head. "No. I used to live all the way over in Murray Hill. It's going to take you an hour to get there from here. At least."

I try to smile. "You can't zap me over to Murray Hill?"

"It doesn't work that way," Adam says. "The wormhole seems to transport things to just outside my house, although I'm not sure why there's that geographical displacement. Anyway, you're going to have to get over there yourself. And I don't think a taxi is a good idea because the money looked different then. I don't have any money from sixteen years ago and I don't want you to get busted for counterfeiting."

"Oh, great," I say. "So I get to walk all the way downtown and cross town?" At least it will save me a trip to the gym. These pancakes aren't doing anything to help my perpetual diet.

"You can probably take the bus," Adam says. "The difference in the coins won't be picked up. That was before everyone had Metrocards too, so you won't look like a freak with a handful of change."

"Right," I say, remembering how annoying it used to be to have to gather two dollars' worth of change to ride the bus. "And when I see you, how will I recognize you?"

Adam frowns. "It's me. Why wouldn't you recognize me?"

"Well, you were only twenty-two then …"

"Oh, I get it," he says with a wry smile. "Because I look fucking fifty now. Is that it?"

I look down at the table. Yeah, that's exactly what I meant.

"You'll recognize me," he says. "Just look out for a dorky guy coming out of my old building, trying to ride a bike in his work clothes."

"Fine," I say. "And how am I supposed to convince you not to ride your bike? Should I tell you that I'm from the future?"

"No, don't do that!" Adam says, looking horrified, even though I was partially kidding.

"Why not?"

"Someone from the past learning about the presence of a time machine could create a rip in the wormhole," he explains.

Say what? I have no idea what he's talking about, and he can tell from my face.

"It could destroy the universe," he clarifies.

Okay, don't tell past Adam about time

machine because it might destroy the universe. Important safety tip. Thanks, Adam. "Great," I say.

"It might not be the whole universe," he says quickly. "Maybe only our own galaxy would be destroyed."

"What a relief." I play with a salt shaker on the table, thinking about the possibility of the universe being destroyed. Or maybe just our own galaxy. I'm starting to lose my nerve, so I push the thought out of my mind and take a deep breath. "So," I say, "if I can't tell you about the time machine, how am I supposed to convince you not to get on the bike?"

He shrugs. "I don't know. Just say to me that I shouldn't ride my bike that day."

I love how Adam has planned this all out to the extent of building a freaking time machine, yet when he has absolutely no clue how to proceed with getting his younger self not to ride a bike. "And you think you'll just listen to that?"

"Yeah, I will."

"And why?"

Adam's cheeks color slightly. "Because I'll think you're pretty."

I wonder if he's right. Almost-forty Adam is certainly smitten with me, but I can't necessarily say the same for twenty-two-year-old Adam. I'm not exactly a young girl. I may look good for my age, but my extra pounds and gravity have definitely taken a toll. And let's face it—twenty-two-year-old Adam is not disabled and probably doesn't have that much difficulty getting attractive women his own age. I don't know if he's going to bend over backwards to do whatever I want.

Then again, I have to trust Adam on this one. After all, who knows him better than himself?

ADAM'S GUIDE TO
WHAT TO DO IF YOU'RE SENT BACK TO PREHISTORIC TIMES

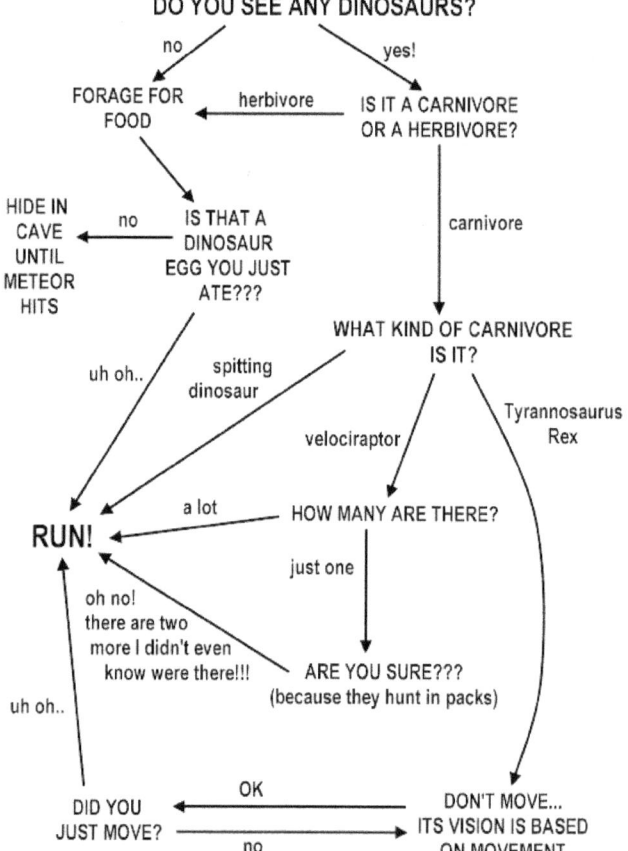

DO YOU SEE ANY DINOSAURS?

no

yes!

FORAGE FOR FOOD

herbivore

IS IT A CARNIVORE OR A HERBIVORE?

HIDE IN CAVE UNTIL METEOR HITS

no

IS THAT A DINOSAUR EGG YOU JUST ATE???

carnivore

WHAT KIND OF CARNIVORE IS IT?

uh oh..

spitting dinosaur

Tyrannosaurus Rex

velociraptor

RUN!

a lot

HOW MANY ARE THERE?

just one

oh no! there are two more I didn't even know were there!!!

ARE YOU SURE??? (because they hunt in packs)

uh oh..

OK

DID YOU JUST MOVE?

no

DON'T MOVE... ITS VISION IS BASED ON MOVEMENT

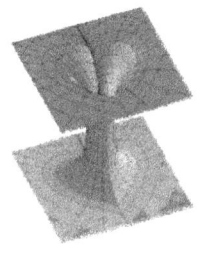

Seven

When we get back to Adam's house, there's nothing left to do but time travel.

Up until this moment, I've somehow managed not to think about it too much and exactly what it will entail, but now that it's going to happen more imminently, I'm getting scared. Yes, Albert the rabbit seems fine, but newsflash: I'm not a rabbit. I can think of any number of things that could go wrong, ranging from being trapped in the year 1997 forever to my own death. It's not all sunshine and rose petals dating an inventor, as it turns out.

"You're sure you want to do this?" Adam asks me for what seems like the millionth time.

"Stop asking me that," I say as I hug my arms to my chest. I'm wearing a hooded sweatshirt because of how cold it was when Albert made his journey, but I still have goose bumps up and down my arms. I can feel all the little hairs standing up on my legs, making my snug blue jeans feel uncomfortable. I just want to get this over with.

"Sorry," he says, and he turns back to the computer screen. "Okay, so I'm setting the time you're going back to as September 23, 1997 at six a.m. That should leave you lots of time to get to Murray Hill. And I'll set it so that you'll stay there for three hours."

Adam wrote down his old address for me, and even his old phone number, just in case. I won't be able to call him from my cell phone, since I don't think smart phones worked back then. But maybe I can find a payphone. Were there still payphones in 1997? I haven't seen any in ages.

"Okay," Adam says again. "Now all you need to do is hop up on the step." Hop on the step? Does he think he's still working with rabbits?

After hesitating a beat longer than necessary, I get onto the step, positioning my feet about eight inches apart.

"Now don't move," he warns me.

I stare at him. "What happens if I move?"

He shrugs. "I don't know. Something bad, maybe."

Something bad, maybe? Are you freaking

kidding me?

It's not too late to change my mind. I don't have to do this. I don't have to be the first human subject for my boyfriend's crazy invention. But when I look at his face, I know that I kind of do. He needs me to do this for him.

"How will I know when I'm going to transport back to 2013?" I ask. "Like, will I sense it?"

Adam shrugs again, this time a little sheepishly. "I figure you can tell me when you get back."

Half-baked. This is so half-baked. I almost want to cry. "Let's just do this," I say. Before I change my mind.

I expect Adam to ask me one more time if I really want to do this, and if he did, I'd probably hop right off the step and go scurrying away. But he doesn't. He reaches out and clicks on ENTER WORMHOLE.

I hear that toilet whooshing noise, now so loud that my ears start to ache and pop. The room starts spinning, my feet feel like they're leaving the ground, and I'm vaguely reminded of the one and only time I tried acid when I was in college. The combination of sensations doesn't make me feel great. In fact, I feel a violent urge to throw up. What happens if you throw up in a wormhole? I can't even imagine, but as Adam said, "something bad, maybe." So I try to push down the urge.

Gradually, the whooshing gets softer and the world stops spinning. I'm on solid pavement again. And the first thing I do is lean over and vomit on the sidewalk.

I feel remarkably better after that, although now that I'm not a college student, it's a little embarrassing to leave behind a little puddle of vomit on the sidewalk. Oh, well, it's not like anyone saw it.

The brisk September air helps my nausea and vertigo as well. When I left 2013, it was June and getting muggy. Now it's breezy and pleasant. I'm so glad Adam got injured in such nice weather. I pat down my body from my head to my toes and discover everything is still intact. Thank God. I zip up my hoodie sweatshirt, and wipe my mouth with the back of my hand. I wish Adam had given me a mint to take with me.

1997. I've traveled to 1997.

Or have I? Honestly, 1997 looks an awful lot like 2013.

I spot a newsstand on the corner and trot towards it. The newsie sees me and gives me a little wave, which I return shakily. The stand smells like ink and cigarettes, which makes my stomach turn slightly. I nearly back away, but before I do, I look down at a fresh newspaper lying in a pile, still bound with twine. I see President Bill Clinton's face smiling up at me in black and white ink. The date on the paper is September 23, 1997.

Holy shit. He did it. The smart bastard actually sent me back to 1997.

I look at my watch, which Adam set for me to correspond to the time in 1997. It's now just after six a.m., so I have plenty of time, but I don't want to mess this up. I've got to find the nearest bus and get my butt to Murray Hill. But before that, I use some of the change Adam gave me to buy a package of breath mints. Because no matter how "pretty" I am, twenty-two-year-old Adam isn't going to like me if my breath smells like puke.

He was right about the bus accepting my change, no problem. As I head downtown, I can't help but think how similar yet different 1997 looks compared to 2013. It's the little differences, you know?

Like for example, nobody is wearing skinny jeans. If this were 2013, all the young girls would be wearing those skintight tapered jeans, even though I'm convinced those jeans don't look good on anyone. I hate skinny jeans. If you have even an ounce of body fat, you look like a cow in those things—and I've got a little bit more than an ounce on my legs. Plus I'm way too old to even attempt to pull it off. But now, everyone's got boot-cut jeans like me. Definitely an improvement.

Also, in 2013, everyone on the bus would be on their phones. Everyone would be texting, playing games, sending emails, surfing the web. Now nobody is doing that. Everyone is just … looking at each other. Or reading books. On paper. Or the newspaper, also on paper. It's so weird.

When I get to 34th Street, I get on the crosstown bus using a transfer. Like I have to hand the driver a piece of paper saying I was on the other bus and I'm transferring to this bus. It's so retro! Really, I don't miss 1997. Well, aside from the fact that I was twenty years old in 1997. I kind of miss that part.

I spot Adam's old building from the bus and I hit the button for it to stop. Naturally, it misses my stop, and I have to hoof it one avenue block back to where I was. On the way, I pass a Borders Bookstore, which I stare at in amazement. A real bookstore, geez. I used to love browsing bookstores, pulling titles off the shelves and plopping down on a beanbag chair to skim the first few pages. I'm a little tempted to go inside, but I can't very well tell Adam that I missed him because I was eating biscotti at Borders.

I park myself on the steps of a brownstone next to Adam's building. There's a huge green awning sticking out with the building number inscribed on it in white script. There are half a dozen steps to the front door, and a ramp beside the steps. My eyes automatically focus in on the ramp until I remember that twenty-two-year-old Adam didn't need ramps. Although he's got his bike, so maybe he does.

It's still well before eight, and I'm beginning to really miss my phone. Honestly, you don't realize how much smart phones have revolutionized our lives. Back in the nineties, if you were waiting for someone, all you could do was … wait.

So I start fantasizing a little bit. I imagine coming back to the future after successfully achieving my mission. I'm having trouble imagining Adam being out of the wheelchair, but I can clearly see how happy his face will be. How grateful he'll be to me. I imagine him taking my hand and pulling a little velvet box out of his pocket. And this time the box won't just have earrings in it.

I've been sitting there for at least forty-five minutes, scrutinizing everybody who came in or out of the building, when I finally see a guy come out lugging a bike, bouncing it down the stairs rather than bothering with the ramp. I squint at him a little and my heart starts pounding in my chest. It's him. It's Adam.

And he's *young*. Oh my God, is he young. He's got his helmet hanging from the handle of his bike and I can see there isn't a thread of gray in his slightly shaggy dark brown hair. He's a little too dorky to be handsome, but he's definitely really, really cute. As promised, he's wearing a white dress shirt rolled up to his elbows and khaki slacks for work, and he's got his pants tucked into his white tube socks. I love how he doesn't give a shit if he looks like a complete doofus.

And he's walking. There's that too. His hips, knees, and ankles bend and move like he's not even thinking about it, which I guess he isn't. It's never even occurred to Adam that walking is something special, something he might not always be able to do. He has no idea what's about to happen to him.

Except it isn't going to happen. I'm going to stop it.

I've had the last forty-five minutes to think about what to say to him, but all my ideas sound terribly stupid as I take big strides in his direction. He's bent over his bike, adjusting the seat, as I stand in front of him. I clear my throat. "Um, hi."

Adam lifts his eyes to look at me, lowers them again, then does a double-take. A slow smile spreads across his face as he straightens up. I can't help think about the first time Adam and I met, a year ago at that dinner party. He did the same thing—the double-take followed by the slow smile. I guess even though I'm old and fat, he still thinks I'm pretty.

"Hello," he says back.

I swallow. Up close, Adam seems even younger. He has no lines on his face. None! Well, maybe one or two at the corner of his eyes (still behind wire-rimmed glasses) when he smiles, but that's it. And he's so tall! How did I never realize how tall he is? I look down and see that he's missed two buttons on his shirt. I guess some things don't change.

"Listen," I say, wringing my hands together, "this is going to sound really weird, but …"

Adam raises his eyebrows at me.

"I'm psychic," I blurt out.

"Psychic," Adam repeats. I'm certain he doesn't believe in such things, but he's still got that amused smile on his lips. I'm getting the feeling that I could say pretty much anything and he'd still keep on smiling like that.

"Just an amateur psychic," I babble on. God, this is awful. I'm not going to convince him of anything. My boyfriend is going to get hit by a taxi today because I'm the worst liar on the face of the planet. "I don't have, like, an office or do professional readings or anything."

"Right …" Adam says. He cocks his head to one side.

"So the thing is," I go on, "I had this premonition. About you."

"About me?" Adam stares at me in

amazement.

"Yes," I say, trying to look confident. "The thing is, you can't ride your bike today. Because if you do, something terrible will happen. To you." I take a deep breath and conclude: "So you can't ride your bike today."

Adam looks at me, looks down at his bike, then back at me. "Okay," he finally says.

I let out the breath I'd been holding. "Okay?"

He shrugs. "Sure. I mean, if you had a *premonition* and all, better be safe than sorry, right?"

I don't think he believes me in the slightest. But as the older Adam had suspected, he's doing it for me because he thinks I'm pretty. Even though I am way, way (way) too old for him.

"I'll leave the bike in the lobby, okay?" he says to me. "I'll take the subway to work."

"Great," I say.

"Just one condition," he says, and that smile returns to his face. He's too adorable for his own good. "You have to let me treat you to a cup of coffee."

I guess I should have seen this coming, but I didn't. I just stare at him, unsure what to say.

"It's the least I can do," he points out to me. "I mean, you saved my life."

He's so full of shit. But if I couldn't say no

to older Adam asking me to risk my life, I'm probably not going to be able to refuse young Adam asking me out to coffee. Anyway, it's not possible to cheat on your boyfriend with himself. I think that's a general rule of time travel.

"Okay," I say.

Adam grins at me. Damn, he is young. I really feel like a cougar, even though in reality he was born two years before I was. "I'm going to put my bike in the lobby. Promise me you won't go anywhere?"

"I promise."

Adam hops up the steps to his building with his bike. God, he is limber. He's one of those guys who always climbs steps two at a time—never would have thought it. How does he have so much energy? It's almost exhausting to watch. Honestly, it's too bad that I have less than an hour left before I go back to 2013. This situation could get pretty interesting.

When Adam returns, he's untucked his pants from his socks, and he's got this big eager grin on his face. He hops down the steps of his building again two at a time and lands right next to me with a resounding thump. "I'm Adam, by the way," he says.

"I know," I say. "I'm psychic, remember?"

"Oh, right," he laughs. "So what's my last name then, Psychic Girl?"

"Schaffer," I say.

That wipes the smile off his face. He squints at me. "Do I know you from somewhere?"

Yeah, from sixteen years in the future. "No."

"What's your name?" he asks.

I can't tell him my real name. I didn't think this situation would come up, so I say the first name that pops into my head: "Tina."

"Cute," he says. "You look like a Tina." I look at his face and I can't help but wonder if this Adam is as good at eating girls out as his future counterpart. Probably not. He's much younger and less experienced, and also he doesn't really need to be good at it. The lower half of his body isn't paralyzed, after all. And it never will be, thanks to me.

Of course, I can't help but wonder if he'll still be good at going down on me when I return to 2013. Maybe he won't. Maybe he'll hate it. Maybe it'll be one of those things he'll only be willing to do on Valentine's Day and my birthday.

That would be a huge loss. But I guess it's selfish to be thinking that way.

"So where are we going?" I ask Adam, as he takes long strides toward the crosswalk.

"I thought you're psychic," he says, winking at me.

"Being psychic doesn't work that way," I

explain, rather lamely.

"Got it," Adam says. He points across the street, to a small café. "They have great coffee there. And whatever else you'd like."

When he says "whatever else you'd like," he's referring to *food*. I'm assuming. Still, my heart speeds up a notch.

The light turns green, and Adam marches into the crosswalk. But before I can follow him, a yellow taxi appears out of nowhere and slams into him. I watch in horror as Adam's body goes flying like a rag dog at least ten feet as the taxi screeches to a halt. Adam lies on the pavement, completely motionless.

I can't freaking believe that just happened.

A crowd has already formed by the time I race over to Adam's body. Is he *dead*? Did my saving him from being hit on his bike mean that he'd get killed as a pedestrian? I push my way through the crowd, falling to my knees beside him, barely even noticing how the gravel cuts into my skin through my jeans. There's blood on his face, but I can't figure out where he's bleeding from. But then he groans and I know he's still alive. For now.

"Adam," I whisper, taking his hand in mine. Please don't die. Please …

I hear sirens in the distance. And then I hear something else, a familiar whooshing noise.

And I realize that I'm seconds away from disappearing. "Nobody move him!" I warn the people surrounding him, but even my voice seems to be fading.

I release Adam's hand and back away from the crowd. There are so many people around, but nobody's paying much attention to me when Adam is half-dead on the street. I grab onto a blue mailbox and crouch down as the world starts to spin. I feel sick, so sick ... and then ...

I'm gone.

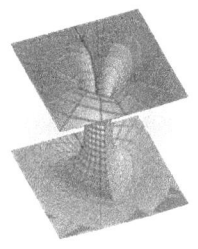

Eight

Adam's living room comes back into focus. I stand still as long as I possibly can because I don't want "something bad" to happen, but as soon as everything seems steady, I collapse onto the floor. I retch somewhat unattractively, but at least I don't throw up this time. I guess I already emptied my stomach.

I lift my head and see that Adam is next to me. He's alive — thank God! Thank God, thank God. I was so scared that he ... well, I don't even want to think about it.

And he's still in his wheelchair, which comes as both a relief and a deep disappointment. I look up at his face and see the same lines around his eyes, the same gray hairs, but something is different about him somehow. I can't quite put my finger on it. "Claudia," he says, wheeling over to me. He puts his hand on my shoulder. "Are you okay?"

I nod, getting unsteadily to my feet. I look around the room. Everything looks exactly the same as when I left, right down to the yellow mustard stain on Adam's ratty couch. All the same. Yet I look back at Adam and I still get that sense he's different somehow, but I still can't say what it is. It's driving me crazy.

Adam looks up at me, shifting in his wheelchair. "So, um, what happened? I thought you were going to stop me from walking in front of that taxi?"

"No," I say. "I was supposed to keep *your bike* from getting hit by a taxi. And I did."

Adam stares at me. "What are you talking about? My bike? I wasn't on a bike."

"You *were*," I insist. "That's what you told me. Keep you from getting on a bike so you wouldn't get hit by a car. And I did!"

"What?" Adam blinks at me. "You ... I never ..."

We stare at each other for a minute, then Adam looks down at his legs. "Maybe," he says, heaving a sigh, "you can't change the outcome. Maybe the future is unchangeable."

I don't know what to say to that. I mean, I did what he wanted me to do. I risked my life going through a goddamn wormhole so he'd be able to walk again, and now he's saying that it didn't matter? That there was no way I could change anything?

"But I *did* change things," I point out. "You were supposed to get hit on your bike and … I changed that part."

"Fantastic," Adam snorts. "I'm still fucking paralyzed." He rubs his face, as if trying to push out the reality of what's happening right now. All his hopes were apparently pinned on this time machine and fixing what happened to him all those years ago.

And that's when I realize what's different about Adam. He's always been a bit lackadaisical about shaving, to the point where I've rarely seen him without some degree of beard growth on his chin. Now he's got about a day's worth of stubble, but even through the mix of gray and brown hairs on his face, I can see a two-inch scar running along his jawline.

Without thinking, I reach out to graze the scar with my fingertips. Adam jerks away from me, frowning. "What are you doing?"

"That scar …" I murmur. "How did you get it?"

He furrows his brow. "What are you talking about? I broke my jaw when the taxi hit me. I told you that." Adam blanches as the realization dawns on him. "Are you saying that before you went back, that scar wasn't there?"

I nod.

Adam's eyes turn glassy. "My jaw was shattered, Claudia. It was wired shut for *two months*. I couldn't eat. I had to drink my meals through a freaking straw. It took almost a year before I could even eat without it hurting when I tried to chew. It *still* hurts sometimes when the weather is bad." He shakes his head. "And you're saying that didn't happen until you went back and tried to fix things?

I swallow. "Uh. I guess so."

Now he's the one who looks like he's going to throw up. "Jesus Christ," he finally says.

My sentiments exactly.

***

For the rest of the day, I can tell Adam is trying to pretend like what happened doesn't matter, like he doesn't care that no matter what I do in that time machine, he'll never walk again. But it's clear he does care. We eat a quiet dinner in his house, which I cooked. It's mac and cheese from a box, which is pretty much the only dish I can manage to not screw up. But I still manage to overcook the noodles, which are all soggy. It's barely edible, which isn't such a bad thing considering it's obvious neither of us feels very hungry.

"I hear all this great stuff about stem cells," I say, trying to perk Adam up. "I mean, it's not like there's no hope. All this stem cell research …"

"Not in my lifetime," Adam mumbles, not lifting his eyes from his cheesy dinner. He makes circles in the pile of noodles with his fork.

"You're not *that* old," I say, trying to tease him, but he doesn't smile. Okay, new tactic: "Listen do you want me to try again? I mean, maybe I should tell you to just not even leave your house that day? You can't get hit by a taxi if you don't go outside, right?" I really don't want to, but I'll do it. For him. If he needs me to.

Adam shakes his head emphatically. "No way. I spent months with my jaw wired shut, which apparently wouldn't have even happened if you hadn't tried to help me. If you go back again, I'll probably end up blind and deaf or something. No thanks. A disfiguring scar is bad enough."

Admittedly, it doesn't sound so great having a jaw wired shut, but I have to take exception to his use of the term "disfiguring scar." The scar on Adam's jaw is, in fact, incredibly sexy. He's always been a bit of a dork and this scar gives him a new, somewhat rugged edge. I want to tell him that, but I have a feeling he'll just think I'm patronizing him.

"Well, look on the bright side," I say in an overly chipper voice. "If you weren't in a wheelchair, you'd have to re-modify your whole house. I don't know if you realize how back-breaking it is to use your sink if you're standing up. And you're much taller than I am."

Adam lifts his eyes from his plate to stare at me. "Claudia, seriously. This isn't helping."

I grit my teeth. "Well, what do you want me to say? Is the only way you can ever be happy is if you're able to walk?"

"No!" Adam says, dropping his fork onto his plate with an echoing clatter. "That's not it at all. I've been in this wheelchair for sixteen years and … well, I guess I'm used to it by now. It's not even that. It's everything that happened between then and now. All that pain. I was hoping that when you went back, it would just be … erased."

He's talking, of course, about The Bitch. That girl who ripped his heart to shreds. Who made it so that every subsequent girl would always be The Other Girl. Even me, apparently.

"I'm sorry," Adam says quietly. "You're so great, Claudia. You deserve a guy who's totally amazing, not some messed up cripple who can't even commit to you."

I wish I could fix this for him. I see the pain on his face, etched into the lines on his skin, and I want desperately to change the past for him. I look across the room at my step, lying abandoned on the floor, still hooked up to the laptop computer, and I wonder if maybe it's not too late. Maybe there really is a way to change the past.

A few years after his injury, Adam met a beautiful girl named Jessica who messed him up big time, and he hasn't ever recovered from it. You can pay for all the therapy you want, but the best thing would be if he never met The Bitch to begin with. As my mother always said, an ounce of prevention is worth a pound of cure.

And that's how I get the idea.

Nine

My plan is pretty brilliant if I do say so myself.

Adam's life got wrecked when he met The Bitch. She found him when he was vulnerable, never having had a relationship since his injury. If he never meets The Bitch, then maybe he won't be so bitter about relationships now.

But how do I stop him from meeting The Bitch?

And this is the brilliant part:

Really, what young Adam needed was a *nice* girl to counteract her influence. And fortunately, there was a very nice girl running around New York in the late nineties. Her name was Claudia.

This is my plan:

Go back in time again while Adam is asleep. Luckily, the machine seems pretty user-friendly and I've watched him work it twice now. I need to find young Adam and young me, introduce them, and watch them fall madly in love. The Bitch will never have a chance. Then I come back to the present, and Adam and I will probably already be married. We'll probably be living in suburbia and have three beautiful children: two girls and a little boy. And a dog named Spot.

Brilliant, right?

There are a few details here and there that I need to work out. First of all, I can't just go for a few hours, because it'll take time to even find Adam and my younger self, and then even more time to ensure that they fall in love. I'm thinking … two weeks. How long does it take two people to fall in love anyway? I know the first time Adam laid eyes on me, he was smitten, and when I met him, I felt the same way. So I'd imagine it will be pretty quick. Maybe I'll even have time to take in a movie or two. Too bad I've seen them all.

If I'm going to the past, when my money and credit cards will be no good, I need a place to crash. Fortunately, my parents have been vacationing in Florida every Christmas holiday for about two or three weeks since I was eighteen, my father's only vacation the whole year. And they haven't changed the locks to their Manhattan apartment in over twenty years. So If I plan for December 26 or thereabouts, I can stay at my parents' apartment without anyone being the wiser.

Then there's the question of what year to return to. I know Adam met The Bitch a few years after his injury, so I don't want to wait too long. Then again, I don't want to catch him when he's still recovering. I finally settle on 1999, just over two years after he got hit by the car. The only negative is that it means I'll probably have to hear that "Tonight we're going to party like it's 1999" song again. I thought I'd never have to hear that song ever again.

With my plan about as settled as it can be, I wait until Adam is asleep in bed to put it into place. Adam is naturally a very restless sleeper, but I can tell he took a sleeping pill tonight, because he's sleeping like the dead. I can hear his deep breathing, an almost-snore, as his chest moves up and down. Adam looks very peaceful when he's in a drugged sleep. Almost like the young Adam I met in 1997. Watching him sleep makes me even more determined to fix his life.

I grab a tote bag from Adam's closet and pack all the clean clothes from the drawer Adam gave me in his dresser. I also grab one of his coats because December in New York is pretty nippy. I'm not going to be the height of fashion on this trip, but that's okay. I'm going to help foster young love, not to hook up with some dude from 1999.

I take a handful of change that's scattered on top of Adam's dresser (his official place for change). I'll want to take a bus across town to my parents' apartment in east midtown. Luckily, they don't have a doorman, so my keys will open the door to the building, and I don't have to worry about some nosy guy wondering why the Williams's daughter has suddenly aged fourteen years.

Adam has left the time machine turned on. Or at least, the laptop is on. I approach slowly, clutching the tote bag in my hand. Am I seriously going to do this? Now that I'm actually standing here, it seems incredibly risky and very unlike me. But on the other hand, it's very romantic. I'm traveling through time to get the young versions of ourselves to fall in love.

Screw it, I've already gone this far. I may as well do it.

I stand in front of the laptop to adjust the settings. I'm going back to December 26, 1999, so I'll miss the Christmas holidays. Two o'clock in the afternoon sounds about right. And I'll stay for two weeks. My finger hovers over the button that says ENTER WORMHOLE. Once I click on that, there's no turning back. I'll be stuck in 1999 for two weeks.

But like I said, screw it.

I click on the button and quickly stand up as straight as I can, doing my best to stand perfectly still so "something bad" doesn't happen. The whooshing noise starts up and I'm suddenly seized by the fear that I've done something wrong. Like, maybe there's some other button I was supposed to click on, or else I'll get sent back to the time of dinosaurs. I don't want to get smooshed by a T. rex. Also, I've heard bad things about velociraptors. What if I get hunted by a pack of 'raptors?

Nah, that doesn't seem too likely.

The spinning starts and that horrible vertigo overtakes me. Thank God I had the presence of mind to bring my mints with me this time, because I will definitely need them.

A minute later, I come to a shaky halt outside Adam's house and I immediately throw up. Talk about déjà vu. I wonder if the person who cleans it up will remember there was vomit in this exact spot two years previously. Unlikely.

I stare up at the brownstone, wondering if Adam lives here yet. Obviously, he can't manage the steps to the front door, so he always goes in through the side entrance, which has no steps. I creep around the side, looking for signs of his wheelchair tracks, but I don't see any. Maybe he still lives in Murray Hill. God, I hope it doesn't take like two weeks to even find him. That would be disappointing. Why didn't I ask Adam where he lived in 1999?

Young Claudia, at least, will be easy to find. She's got an apartment in the East Village and works as a waitress in a restaurant that specializes in chicken dishes. It's called Plucky's. It closed about ten years ago, due to the high rates of salmonella poisoning in customers. (If you live in 1999, don't eat at Plucky's.)

I reach my parents' apartment in record time and see how little it's changed in the last fourteen years. The main difference is how painfully out of date their old television and computer look. The screen on their desktop is laughably small. It's sort of like when you're watching a movie from two decades ago and you're like, "Wow, did computers really used to look like that?"

I creep into my parents' bedroom, where my anal-retentive mother has made the bed prior to leaving for Florida. I open the second drawer in their antique dresser and let out a sigh of relief that my parents haven't changed the hiding place for their extra cash. This stash got me through my tough times in high school and college, and now in my thirties, it's saving my hide.

In the past, I've been careful not to take too much, but this time I help myself to two-hundred dollars. After all, by the time they realize it's missing, I'll be long gone. They're pretty wealthy, so it's not like they'll really care anyway. You have to be wealthy to own a three-bedroom apartment in East Midtown.

The other part of my plan is that I go to the pharmacy downstairs and buy a bottle of chestnut brown hair dye. I know I've aged fourteen years since 1999, but I'm still worried about young Claudia recognizing me and going into shock or something at seeing her older self. Plus now I get to see if brunettes have more fun than blondes. I'm guessing no.

As I spread the brown dye through my hair using my gloved fingers, my eyes watering from the fumes, I wonder if Adam is missing me back in 2013. But no, that doesn't make any sense. Even though it's been a couple of hours here, when I transport back to 2013, it will be only a minute later. He won't even know I've been gone, aside from the fact that if my plan works, his whole life will be different. My life too, maybe.

Once the brown dye is in my hair, I study my reflection in the mirror. It's amazing how much of a difference hair color makes—I look nearly unrecognizable. Moreover, I know I'll look vastly different than I did at age twenty-two. Aside from the extra ten pounds (okay, twenty), my face just looks older. More mature. I don't have many wrinkles, aside from a little groove between my eyebrows and laugh lines that don't fade completely when I stop laughing, but I know I don't look twenty-two. I just don't.

In any case, I'm absolutely certain young Claudia won't recognize me. And I'm sort of hoping Adam won't recognize me either as the person who warned him not to ride his bike and then let him get hit by a taxi anyway.

As I blow-dry my hair, it occurs to me that it would be about two a.m. now if I had stayed in 2013, and I'm completely exhausted. I know I've got a ton of stuff to do, but I'm going to be pretty useless if I don't get some sleep. So I hit up the guest bedroom, and the second my head hits the pillow, I'm down for the count.

***

I dream restlessly. Mostly snippets that I don't remember about the last year of my life with Adam. It's funny how we've only been together a year, yet somehow I feel like I've known him forever.

I met Adam over a year ago, at a dinner party thrown by mutual friends of ours. I had recently broken up with my boyfriend Sam, and I was still smarting from it. Sam was an investment banker, and in retrospect, far too handsome. Everyone warned me that he wasn't the kind of guy who was interested in settling down, and sure enough, he started hinting around at the nine-month mark that he wanted to see other people. When I told him in no uncertain terms that I did *not* want to see other people, he called it quits. Just like that, like the relationship hadn't mattered at all to him.

So I wasn't excited about going to a dinner party with three couples, two of whom were married. I was beginning to feel like that last loser friend who was going to be single forever. Even my friends who were perpetually single in our early thirties were now in long-term relationships. I predicted being at this party was going to make me feel awkward and seventh wheely and ultimately depressed. I nearly canceled a hundred times but finally ended up going because it was better than sitting at home on a Saturday night. Slightly better.

I definitely wasn't expecting to meet anyone at the party, although when you're single, you're always sort of thinking you might meet someone. Like I'd go out to the grocery store to buy a carton of low fat milk and I'd put on some lipstick, thinking maybe I'd meet someone. (For the record, I never met a guy at the grocery store in my life.) That's the one thing that I enjoyed about being single — the possibilities.

Of course, as soon as I got to the party, I smelled set-up. Mostly because everyone was just a little too excited to see me. I'm sure I'm great company and all, but my friend Nancy hadn't given me that wide a smile in years.

Another time, I might have been irritated. But I was ready to move on from Sam and I was sick of being single. I just hoped for two things: that he was taller than I was and that he had a decent job.

I'll admit that I wasn't super thrilled when I saw Adam for the first time. When you imagine your dream guy, you probably aren't picturing a wheelchair. I'd never been out with a guy who was disabled before. Actually, scratch that—when I was in my twenties, some busybody set me up on a blind date with a guy in a wheelchair who was developmentally disabled (or whatever the correct term for that is), and I had to sneak out before the appetizers arrived—not my finest moment, that's for sure. But Adam wasn't like that other guy. He was nice-looking, well dressed, and Nancy nudged me and told me he was wealthy, even though I'd told her a million times that I couldn't care less about things like that.

As Nancy whispered Adam's attributes in my ear, he detached himself from the conversation he was having to look in my direction. It was just a glance initially, but then he did a double-take, and a slow smile spread across his lips. He was very sexy when he smiled. It was at that moment that I knew that if he asked me for my number, I'd say yes.

We were seated together quite conspicuously during the dinner. As I settled into the seat next to where Adam's wheelchair was parked, he held out his hand to me. I shook it and was surprised by how rough and calloused his palm was. "I'm Adam," he said. He smiled, and I had to admit, he was incredibly cute. "I don't think we've officially met yet."

I didn't admit that his name had already been murmured in my ear a dozen times since I arrived. "Nice to meet you. I'm Claudia."

"Claudia," he said, letting my name roll over his tongue. "Claudia, I don't mean to alarm you, but I'm pretty sure we're being set up."

"I'm getting that sense as well," I giggled.

"We should get revenge," he said, his brown eyes wide behind his glasses. I tried to pin down his age and my best guess was early forties, but at the same time, there was something youthful about his eyes.

"Any suggestions?"

"We should go out on a date," he said thoughtfully. "That will show them."

"Hmm," I said. "Wouldn't it show them more if we *didn't* go out on a date?"

Adam shook his head. "No, that would only show *me*."

Later, in the kitchen, Nancy gave me the vital stats: Adam was thirty-seven, never married, owned his own house, worked as a computer programmer but was independently wealthy on top of that. "He's such a nice guy,

Claudia," Nancy assured me. A nice guy. I needed one of those. Really, really badly.

So when Adam asked me for my number at the end of the night, I didn't hesitate to say yes.

***

I wake up hours later feeling really disoriented. You know that feeling you get when you fall asleep in an unfamiliar place like a hotel or a boyfriend's house, then wake up and have no idea where you are? Well, imagine you fall asleep in an unfamiliar *year*. Yeah, I'm pretty out of it.

I sit up in the double bed of my parents' guestroom, rubbing my eyes, gathering my thoughts. There's part of me that feels like this has all got to be some sort of crazy dream, but obviously it isn't, because I'm here instead of in Adam's bed. I'm actually doing this.

I hear a crash coming from the living room and I clutch the blankets to my chest. Who's here? Oh, my God, is that my *parents*? Were they so freaked out about Y2K that they decided not to go to Florida in 1999? Is that possible? Am I about to spend the next two weeks in jail for breaking and entering?

In any case, I'm on the fifteenth floor, so there's absolutely no way I can escape through the window or something like that. So as quietly as I can, I tiptoe out into the hallway to investigate.

There are two people in the kitchen, a boy and a girl. They're rifling through the cupboards, pulling out seasoning and pasta. The girl is laughing as the boy tries to kiss her and she pushes him away then finally acquiesces.

I know who they are. The boy is Jed Morton. He's just as tall and lanky as I remembered him, his long brown hair hanging loose around his face. Jed Morton, drummer for Snugglepuss, a name that will likely go down as the worst band name in the history of the world. He's also a waiter. He also cheated on me with a stripper named Crystal-Joy. You don't forget a name like that.

And the girl, of course, is me.

Apparently, I was going through a Britney Spears "One More Time" phase back then. My ash-blond hair is tied in two messy braided pigtails resting on each shoulder, and I've got on a plaid skirt that's almost short enough to show off my panties. And I'm wearing *so* much black eye make-up that it looks like I smeared it on with my fists. It's almost painful to look at.

It's equally painful to look at my former body. Wow. Is it possible I really used to look like that? My thighs are so thin and toned, without an ounce of cellulite to be found, even though I know for a fact that I never went to the gym. My waist is so trim and my boobs are so ... high. They're perfect. The most perfect breasts I've ever seen.

I look down at my own breasts, secured with supportive underwire, and I almost cry.

I'm so busy thinking about my breasts that I don't watch what I'm doing and slip against the wall. The couple looks up at me in surprise. Jed doesn't look too concerned but young Claudia quickly brandishes a spatula in a very threatening way and edges toward me. She eyes my face and I hope to God she doesn't recognize me. "Who are you?"

I raise my hands up in the air to show I don't have any weapons. "I'm your cousin. Your parents ... Marge and Don ... they said that I could stay here while they're in Florida. They gave me a key."

Claudia looks me up and down, her blue eyes filled with suspicion. "What cousin? I don't remember you, and you don't look like you're related to me."

"Sure she does," Jed pipes up. Even though he's sticking up for me, I still want to punch him in his handsome face. Really, I can't believe he cheated on me with a stripper. Or he *is going* to cheat on me. "You guys have the same nose and eyes."

"I don't see it," Claudia says, squinting at me. "What's your name?"

"I'm Beth," I say, sticking with my pattern of four letter names. "I'm your second cousin. Sue and Steve's daughter."

Steve is my father's cousin and Sue is his wife. I have no idea if they have a daughter named Beth, but the good thing about that is that I'm pretty sure that Claudia doesn't know either. In any case, the lie works. She lowers the spatula, her shoulders relaxing. "Oh, okay," she says. "Sorry about that."

"No problem," I say, shrugging like I didn't just about have a heart attack. My left arm almost feels like it's tingling.

"Do you have any plans for your trip, Beth?" Jed asks me. He's leering at me and it's making me uncomfortable. I know I said there was that rule about how you can't technically cheat on a person with their younger or older self, but I think the rule is voided if you don't know it's the same person. And Jed definitely doesn't realize I'm an older version of his girlfriend.

"Well, it's my first time in New York," I lie, "so I figured I'd just try to, you know, soak up some culture."

"You should come hear Jed's band play tonight," Claudia says, her eyes widening with excitement. She's very friendly now that she doesn't think I'm an intruder, although in all honesty, she's not the kind of person I'd want to befriend these days. I really just want to grab a tissue and dab off some of that black make-up. Claudia, you're making me look like a whore.

"You're in a band?" I say to Jed, trying to look surprised. "Wow. What's it called?"

"Snugglepuss," Claudia says because Jed is too embarrassed. Rightfully so. "They sound just like Limp Bizkit, only more edgy."

"Snugglepuss?"

"It's the brand name of our lead singer's girlfriend's vibrator," Jed explains, turning slightly red. Seriously, I can't imagine finding your girlfriend's vibrator in a drawer and saying, "Hey, what a great name for my band!"

"Interesting," I say. I really don't want to listen to Jed's band's cacophonous music, but then again, this will give me a chance to talk to Claudia. I have to convince her to dump Jed's ass and go out with a nice guy like Adam instead. Actually, this will be great. If Claudia dumps Jed now, I can spare her (me) being cheated on. "All right, I'm game."

"Sweet!" Jed says, which reminds me how long it's been since I've heard someone call something "sweet."

"Also," Claudia says to me. "There's kind of a particular way people dress at these places." She looks me up and down. "Maybe I can lend you some of my clothes. What size are you?"

It takes all my self-restraint to keep from glaring at her. No, I am not the same size I was when I was twenty-two. Who is? "Size eight," I say.

"Oh, sorry," Claudia says. "My stuff is probably going to be way too small on you."

Yeah. Thanks.

She's right though.

"I guess what you're wearing now is fine," she says. "Just let me help you with your make-up. I bet I can make you look totally cute."

I know I said I wanted kids with Adam, but right now, I really don't want to have a daughter.

***

As I expected, Claudia and I nearly come to blows over the make-up. She's got the full line of Revlon products, but in colors that are just way too vivid. Over the years, I've changed my make-up style to be more subtle than in the old days. I mean, when you're a first grade teacher, you can't walk around looking like a clown. But I guess you can if you're a waitress at Plucky's. It's almost encouraged.

"This black eyeliner will really bring out your eyes," Claudia insists. She looks like she's about to stab me in the eye with it.

"It's okay, really," I say.

Claudia puts her hands on her hips. "Just because you're forty, Beth, it doesn't mean you have to look it."

"I'm not forty," I say through my teeth.

Claudia looks at me sideways. "Really? Older or younger?"

I am beginning to hate this girl, I really am.

Claudia insists on my putting on a thin layer of eyeliner and it doesn't look too bad. I still think it's too much for my age, but I know that I'm definitely not going to run into my employer here. It would actually be a good time to cut loose a little if I didn't have an important plan I had to carry out.

Claudia actually looks pretty amazing. Even though she's wearing far too much make-up, somehow it suits her. She's ditched the Britney Spears look for fishnet stockings, black leather boots, and a short leather skirt. It's almost too much, but somehow she manages to pull it off and looks great. I'm getting incredibly jealous of myself here.

Snugglepuss is playing at a seedy bar in the village, which is filled with the smell of cigarettes and cheap beer. Claudia snags us a tiny round table right where the instruments are set up and the thirty-six-year-old in me starts to protest. I don't want to be right up close to the bass and have my ears ringing the whole night. But Claudia doesn't seem to care about that, and also doesn't care that she's damaging the hearing of her future self (me).

I almost choke when Claudia pulls a pack of Virginia Slims out of her purse and lights one up. I completely forgot how I used to smoke back then. I want to rip it right out of her hand, yelling that she is going to have to pay for the tooth whitening I'm going to have to get in a few years. Plus I can just feel the wrinkles forming on my face.

"You really shouldn't smoke," I say to Claudia, unable to stop myself. "It gives you wrinkles and makes your teeth yellow."

"Yes, *mother*," Claudia says.

"I'm serious," I say. "You may be twenty-two now, but you won't be forever. Don't you care about looking young when you're older?"

In answer to my question, Claudia blows smoke in my face. I am beginning to think she's sorry she let me tag along. I'm very tempted to go out and buy her a nicotine patch, but I know she won't appreciate that gesture. I need to try to be her friend, but I can't help wanting to keep her from ruining my body.

I have to try a different tactic with her. Right now, we kind of hate each other, and that's not going to bode well if my goal is to get her to dump Jed and date Adam. She'll probably do the opposite of anything I tell her to do, just out of spite. I have to act less like her mother and more like her cool older sister.

In an attempt to seem casual, I lean my

elbow on the table, which tilts threateningly to one side. I pull my arm away and notice my shirt is sticky where it had been touching the table. In fact, the whole table is sticky and covered in crumbs, but Claudia doesn't seem to care in the slightest. I am way too old to be in a place like this.

"So how long have you been dating Jed?" I ask her.

A dreamy expression comes over her face. I suppose Jed is handsome in a starving musician sort of way, but I honestly can't even remember feeling that way about him. I only hate Jed now. "About six months," she says. "He's crazy sexy, isn't he?"

I shrug. "I guess so. If you're into guys who are broke."

Claudia looks at me sharply. "He's not broke."

"He's not?" I raise my eyebrows at her. "He's a bartender, right? And is he even getting paid for this gig?"

"So what?" Claudia says. "The band is great, and they're totally going to be a huge hit. He's probably going to be a millionaire."

Don't count on it, honey. Actually, I have no idea what Jed is doing in 2013, but I know for a fact that Snugglepuss is not a huge hit, that's for sure.

"Anyway," Claudia says. "Money isn't important to me. I mean, *look* at him."

I'm getting this really bad feeling. If Jed is her ideal guy, then I have no idea how I'm going to sell Adam. Adam is just about the diametric opposite of Jed.

Jed and his band finally come on for their set. I have to admit, I'm beginning to remember what I saw in Jed. I still hate the guy for cheating on me with a stripper, but he's also super hot. He works up such a sweat from drumming that his T-shirt sticks to his skin and I can see the outline of perfect pecs. Adam has a great upper body thanks to all the wheeling, but I think Jed probably still has him beat. I look over at Claudia and she's practically salivating.

This isn't going so well. Claudia has a boyfriend that she's totally infatuated with, and I don't even know where the hell Adam even is. Great.

Hopefully, my luck will turn around real soon.

Snugglepuss Love Song Template

Look into my eyes, [*Girl's name*]

You will see my soul, [*Girl's name rhyme*]

You set me on [*fire synonym*] when you smile

And now I'll [*be here for a while, go into exile, save your photos to a data file*]

I want to feel your [*body part*] against my skin

[*And I want to, But I just can't*] let you in

I'm just going to [*kiss you, make sweet love to you by the fire, break your heart, give you hell*] again

[*And, But*] I just can't bear to [*watch you leave me on a jet plane, give you up to Dane, call your name out in the rain*]

It's a [*cloudy, sunny, beautiful, rainy*] day

But you make me feel [*good, bad, inspired, like a man*] anyway

Chorus

Oh, [*Girl's name*]!

You're my [*Girl's name rhyme*]

(repeat x [*at least 5 times*])

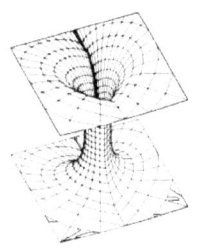

Ten

Considering last night with Claudia was a total loss, when I wake up the next morning, I decide to go at the other end of my plan. Adam. I need to find him.

And no, he's not in the phone book. My parents actually have one and he's not in it.

A few facts I know about Adam Schaffer:

1. He was born and raised in Akron, Ohio, and couldn't wait to get the hell out of there when he turned eighteen.

2. He's the youngest of three kids. He has an older sister Kim and an older brother Ryan. He has a bunch of nieces of nephews, none of whom have apparently

motivated him to want to procreate with me.

3. He has horrible vision. If I'm two feet away from him and he's not wearing his glasses, he literally cannot tell if I'm frowning or smiling.

4. He sings in the shower and is completely off-key.

5. His least favorite food is pickles. If we get fast food burgers, he'll ask for no pickles. And if he ends up with pickles anyway, he'll remove them with a napkin, then fling them in my general direction. (I like pickles.)

None of these factoids are remotely helpful in finding him, unless one of the places I'd been considering looking was a pickle store (it wasn't). It occurred to me that maybe after his accident, Adam had gone back to live with his parents for a while. Then again, I remember him saying that his mother tried to bulldoze him into going back to live at home when he first got hurt, but he couldn't stomach the idea.

So he's probably in the city. Somewhere.

He went back to school to get his Master's in computer science in 2003, so he's probably still working full time at this point. Except where? He's been at his current company for several years, but not since 1999. He was probably working for … some other computer company. So yeah, I have no idea where he works.

In summary, I have no idea where Adam works, I have no idea where he lives, and I have less than two weeks to get him to fall in love with my younger self, who incidentally has a boyfriend.

The good news is that I know Adam is single. It's well known that The Bitch was his first girlfriend after his injury and he won't meet her for another year or two. So I may actually have a chance to convince him to go out with Claudia, who's at least pretty.

I just have to find the guy.

***

I borrow one of my mother's coats because I feel ludicrous in Adam's oversized coat from 2013. I hoof it to Murray Hill and do a little stakeout of Adam's old building, which is pretty much the only place I can think to look. I sit on the steps of the brownstone from two years ago, and watch the entrance of the building for any signs of guys in wheelchairs. But it's freezing out, and I can feel my ears getting frostbitten after about fifteen minutes. I decide to get some sustenance: coffee.

I look around and see that café Adam had pointed out to me two years ago. It's still there.

Yes, I am a little disturbed that he almost died getting coffee from there, but I'm freezing and it's no time to be picky. I go across the street and order myself a cup of decaf.

The café is small and quaint, filled with the thick aroma of roasting coffee beans. There are free tables, and as much as I know I need to go out there and look for Adam, it is really freaking cold outside. I'm sure I won't miss him if I spend fifteen minutes here drinking my piping hot beverage.

The coffee is just as good as Adam had promised it would be. I wrap my fingers around the paper cup, absorbing its warmth. Ah, this is nice. For the first time since I got to this goddamn year, I finally feel relaxed.

That is, until I see Adam come in through the door.

Wheel in, I should say. Unlike last time, he's in a lightweight wheelchair that doesn't look terribly different from the one he uses in 2013. His feet rest quietly on the single footplate and his legs don't move at all, except when they bounce slightly after he wheels over an imperfection in the floor. His hair is cut a little shorter, and he has the same face from two years ago, but something is different somehow. It's hard to put my finger on it—something in his eyes.

"Medium coffee, black," Adam says to the

cashier. He's got leather gloves on his hands, which he pulls off so that he can dig his wallet out of a bag attached to the back of his chair. He seems pretty comfortable with the wheelchair, but then again, it *has* been over two years.

I sink into my own seat, knowing I have to approach him, but half-hoping he won't see me. Maybe he won't recognize me. It *was* over two years ago, we only talked for a brief time, and my hair is a different color. He probably won't have any idea who I am. I'll say I'm Beth and he won't suspect a thing.

Adam grabs the cup of coffee from the cashier and tucks it between his legs. He wheels around and is about to head for the door when his eyes rest on me. He does a double-take, but it's definitely not followed by a smile this time. Adam does not look happy to see me. In fact, I'd say there's a pretty good chance he hates me. In any case, he definitely knows who I am.

"You!" he says, wheeling closer to me.

I blink innocently. "Uh, hi. Adam, right?"

"What are you doing here, Psychic Girl?" he hisses in my direction. I see that underneath the stubble on his chin, he now has that sexy scar along his jawline. "Come to finish me off?"

I grip my coffee cup. "No. I, um …"

Adam is glaring at me, waiting for an answer, an explanation of some sort. I don't blame him. I told him something awful was going to happen if he rode his bike, then something awful happened.

"I'm not really psychic," I say lamely.

"Oh, really?"

"But it's not my fault that taxi hit you," I insist. "I didn't mean for it to happen."

"You know, this is *permanent*," Adam says, waving at his legs. "It's not, like, a broken leg. I'm in a wheelchair for the rest of my life. I'm not going to walk again. Ever."

"I'm sorry," I say quietly.

"Why are you apologizing?" he retorts. "I thought it wasn't your *fault*."

"It wasn't," I say. "But I'm still … sorry."

"I don't need your pity, thanks," Adam says. He takes his coffee cup and places it on the table in front of me. "Don't take this to mean I'm joining you. I just don't want my legs to get scalded. Nice dye job, by the way."

I touch my hair self-consciously then take a sip of my coffee, more to have something to do with my hands than anything else. Adam is continuing to glare at me, and it's pretty uncomfortable. I'm worried he's going to try to have me arrested.

"I actually tried to look for you, you know," he says. "After I got out of the hospital. I wanted to figure out what the hell happened that day. But I didn't have much to go on, aside from the name Tina. That probably isn't even your real name, is it?"

"It's Beth, actually," I say.

"Really? Is that the fake name you're going by now?"

"It's my real name!"

"Yeah, well, how about showing me some ID, *Beth*?"

Okay, he's got me there. He rolls his eyes to demonstrate how unsurprised he is that I'm unable to produce any kind of identification.

"Let me make it up to you," I say.

He leans across the table, staring at me with his nice brown eyes. It's the man I love, but fourteen years younger. He's very sexy, actually. Maybe I really can get young Claudia to fall for him. "You're going to make it up to me?" he growls. "I'm paralyzed for life. What are you going to do? Buy me flowers?"

He's got a point.

"A girl," I say in a hoarse voice. "I'll set you up with a girl."

Adam's brow furrows for a minute. Finally, he laughs. It's not exactly a happy laugh, but it's still a bit of a relief after how angry he was a minute ago. "Yeah, sorry, not interested."

"She's really amazing," I say. "She's twenty-two years old, really beautiful, smart, funny, nice …"

I'm probably laying it on too thick, especially since Claudia isn't exactly all those things. Well, she's twenty-two. And she's very attractive. The rest ... not so much.

"Wow, sounds great," Adam says, an edge of sarcasm in his voice.

"I think you'd really like her," I say.

Adam shakes his head at me. "Sorry, I just don't do that whole ... blind date thing."

He reaches for his cup of coffee and I start to panic. He's going to leave before I convince him to go out with Claudia. This is bad.

"You're not seeing anyone though, right?" I say.

Adam narrows his eyes at me. "No ..."

"So ... don't you want to get back on the horse? Start dating again?"

"That's pretty insulting," Adam says. "You're just assuming I haven't dated any girls since I got hurt."

I look him in the eyes. "Well, have you?" I know he hasn't.

"Right," he grumbles. "I forgot you're psychic. Fine. No girls."

"I'm not psychic, actually."

Adam rolls his eyes again. "You know," he says, "I thought a lot about what would happen if I ever ran into you again. I definitely never thought you'd bulldoze me into going on a blind date."

"I guess you're not psychic, either."

"Guess not."

He stares at me across the table. I can't help but think of what Adam said to me before he sent me back to 1997. *I'll do it because I'll think you're pretty.* Does he still think I'm pretty? Enough so that he'll agree to do what I want?

Adam tugs on his earlobe, the same nervous habit he has in 2013. Another fun fact about my Adam: he goes completely crazy when I suck on his earlobes. I just discovered it by accident once, when I was exploring his upper body, trying to figure out what turned him on the most. As soon as my tongue touched his earlobe, I knew I had hit the money spot. He squirmed and groaned, completely losing control of himself.

As Adam's eyes meet mine, I know he doesn't have a clue what I'm thinking about and I'm very grateful for that. Can you imagine if he knew I was thinking about sucking on his earlobes? That wouldn't do at all.

Anyway, after what feels like an hour, he finally breaks the silence: "This fantastic girl … what's her name?"

"Claudia," I say.

"Claudia?" he snorts. "What is she — French?"

"I think it's a nice name," I say defensively, and he shrugs.

"And she'd be okay with my whole … situation?" Adam asks. His brows knit together and my heart aches just a tiny bit for him. I can see how easy it must have been for The Bitch to break him.

"Absolutely," I say with more confidence than I feel.

"Fine," he says. "I'll do it. You're right about, you know, the horse and all. Getting back on it. I should."

Wow, that was ... well, not *easy*, but not as bad as it could have been. I almost expected to have scalding hot coffee thrown in my face by now.

"So let me get your cell number," I say to Adam.

He stares at me blankly. "My ... what?"

Oh right, hardly anybody had cell phones back in 1999. God, how did we live like that? We were like cavemen. "Your phone number, I mean."

He scribbles it down for me on a napkin and I promise I'll give him a call. Now all I have to do is convince the girl to go out with him.

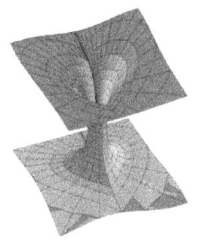

Eleven

I vividly remember my first date with Adam. My Adam, that is.

He called the day after the party where we first met. I recognized his voice right away when he called me. "Adam, right?" I said. I was glad he'd called the next day and hadn't waited the obligatory three days in order to pretend he couldn't care less about me.

"Right!" He sounded really pleased I remembered him. "Okay, how's this? You, me, Indian food, Friday night."

"Sounds great."

We were all set to have dinner that Friday, but there was a meeting at school that ran late and I ended up having to cancel. The second time we were supposed to go out, there was a blizzard, believe it or not. When we talked on the phone to reschedule, I joked, "Maybe it's just not meant to be."

"No," Adam said firmly. "It is meant to be. Let's try again."

Third time was a charm. Adam met me at my building carrying a single rose on his lap. It probably cost a few dollars only, but the gesture really touched me. I also loved that he wore a navy blue tie over his crisp white shirt. It showed that he was making an effort on my behalf. Plus I know how damn uncomfortable ties are, so I felt extra flattered. That said, his shirt was kind of wrinkled, although he at least managed to button it correctly that day.

"So how did Nancy convince you to agree to go out with me?" Adam asked when we were seated in the Indian restaurant. There was a live musician playing some sort of flute in the corner of the room, and Adam had to raise his voice slightly to make himself heard over the music.

I laughed at his question. "You suspect treachery?"

"A little, yes." He smiled and the creases around his eyes deepened.

"She told me you were nice," I said.

"Nice?" He raised his eyebrows. "That's it? That's all it took?"

"She also said you were smart and funny

and …" I hesitated, deciding if I should be honest. "Rich."

I was worried I'd said the wrong thing, but Adam just looked amused. "How rich? Am I, like, a millionaire? Or a billionaire?"

"I don't think you're a billionaire," I said.

"Really? What gave me away?"

"If you were a billionaire," I said, "I think you'd probably be able to get someone to iron your shirts for you."

Adam looked down at his wrinkled shirt and I instinctively reached out and straightened out his collar for him. His cheeks reddened slightly as I did it, but he didn't look upset. He actually looked sort of pleased that I had initiated physical contact. And then after I pulled away, there was this long silence.

"So," I said finally, "what did Nancy say to convince you to go out with me?"

"She told me you were nice," Adam said, grinning at me.

"Oh, please."

"She didn't have to say much," he said. "I mean, she would have had to physically restrain me to keep me from asking you out." He winked at me. "And I'm stronger than I look."

His statement prompted me to check out his biceps. Of course, they weren't easy to see under his shirt, but I later got to see them up close and personal and decided that they were pretty impressive. Like I said, even though he's slim, the muscles in his arms are tight and firm from all his years of wheeling. Adam was right — he's really strong.

I have to admit, the wheelchair thing made me a little uncomfortable at first, which was the reason I'd been so willing to cancel our impending date. I don't know why exactly. I guess it was the fact that I was aware he couldn't stand up and walk, like every other person. He was *disabled*. Like those kids I used to see on the PBS specials when I was younger. I'd never known anyone who was disabled before.

But the truth is, the more we talked, the more I forgot all about it. It was just a chair, after all — it wasn't him. And Adam was really easy to talk to and he had a great sense of humor — and he was incredibly cute. We lost track of time and finally the manager of the restaurant tapped Adam on the shoulder and told us that they were closing for the night.

"Wow," Adam said, looking at his watch. "I didn't realize how late it was."

"I guess we should go," I said, wondering if he'd ask me back to his place, uncertain if I should go. I didn't want the night to end, but I also didn't want him to think I was the kind of girl who went back to a guy's place on a first date.

"Hey, wait," Adam said. Then he grabbed

my shoulders, pulled me close to him, and kissed me gently on the lips. It took me by surprise, but not in a bad way. The stubble on his chin grazed my chin, but his lips were soft, his breath sweet from the wine we'd drunk. "Sorry, I had to do that now. It was going to be much trickier when you stood up."

"No problem," I said, a little breathlessly.

He took me back to my apartment building, but he was a gentleman and didn't ask to come up. And he didn't try to kiss me again, at least not that night.

***

Now that I've got Adam on board with the date, I just have to convince Claudia. And therein lies the real challenge.

A few facts I know about twenty-two-year-old Claudia Williams:

1. She is an only child whose parents dote on her way too much. That is, she's a spoiled brat.

2. She is a size two and I hate her.

3. She was born and raised in Manhattan, attended private schools as well as an expensive private college, all paid for by Mom and Dad. She believes if she lived anywhere but Manhattan, she'd

literally die of cultural shock. Or at least, she pretends to believe that.

4. She is absolutely infatuated with Jed and not because of his sparkling personality.

5. She's not going to shape up and realize she's been wasting her life for at least two more years.

6. In all likelihood, she doesn't deserve a happy ending, but I'm going to try to give it to her anyway.

Claudia is going to be a tough cookie to crack. I can be really stubborn when I want something, and back in 1999, I wanted Jed Morton. Plus I'm pretty sure I thought nobody over the age of thirty was right about anything. And according to Claudia, I'm now like a hundred years old, which is way older than thirty.

The only thing I can think of is that I've got to convince her that there's something terribly wrong with Jed, something that she can't possibly overlook. And I know she's probably willing to overlook a whole lot for a hot body like Jed's, but I'm sure she has *some* standards. (Please, God, let her have some standards.)

Of course, every time she shows up in the apartment, she's with Jed. I've got to catch her when she's alone. And I know exactly where to find her.

***

Plucky's looks just as cheap and awful as I remember it. The owner (and my boss) Devin wanted the place to look classy, but he just didn't achieve it with the big yellow sign with PLUCKY'S written in cartoon red lettering. He also misses the mark with the alternative music station blasting at an ear-shattering volume. The tables are metallic and incredibly tacky, and the whole place smells like grease. Burnt grease.

Plucky's official motto was: "All our dishes have chicken in them!" I really, really hated that motto. Because that pretty much guaranteed, like, twenty comments a day from people who thought they were really clever asking, "Does the bread have much chicken in it?"

No! The bread does not have chicken in it! The water does not have chicken in it! The apple pie does not have chicken in it! (Or if it does, it's just accidental.)

As you can imagine, I don't have great memories of that place.

When I walk into Plucky's, I see Claudia right away. She's wearing her Britney Spears messy pigtail braids, her usual amount of black eye make-up, and the bright yellow T-shirt with

Plucky's printed on it. No bra, of course, because that might keep her nipples from being visible and reduce her tips.

Plucky's is self-seating because Devin is too cheap to hire a hostess, so I slip into the seat of a two-person table and try to catch Claudia's eye. Eventually, she sees me and drags herself over. She has really mastered the bored waitress look. "Hey, Beth," she says. "What can I get for you?"

I reach the menu, but then I remember how I used to intentionally not wash my hands once during my entire shift. "I, uh … I'm not really hungry."

Claudia rolls her eyes. "I can't let you sit here if you don't order something."

"Fine," I say. I glance at the menu and my stomach churns. "I'll have a Diet Coke."

Claudia smirks. "Good choice."

It takes her about twenty minutes to bring me a can of Diet Coke. I knew I was a shitty waitress, but I don't think I ever appreciated how awful I was until this very moment. Oh, well.

After Claudia smacks the drink down on the table in front of me, she starts to walk away. I quickly say, "Wait, Claudia. I need to talk to you."

Really, she should tell me that she's working and doesn't have time to talk, but naturally, she doesn't say that. She leans against the empty chair across from me and smiles. "What's up?"

"It's about Jed," I say. I close my eyes and think of the worst thing that's ever happened to me in a relationship. "You should know that I heard from a very reputable source that Jed … has crabs."

To my surprise, Claudia laughs. "Don't I know it! Don't worry — we both got treated."

Oh, right, *Jed* was the guy who gave me crabs. Asshole.

"Look," I say. "I just think that Jed is wrong for you. I mean, he's such a loser. He's in that dreadful band, which is never going to be successful."

Claudia frowns at me. "What are you talking about? Snugglepuss is awesome. No offense, but you're just too old to get their music."

"No, they're awful," I insist.

"They're great," Claudia insists harder. "And I'll prove it to you." She spots a waitress at the other end of the restaurant and yells out, "Amy! Come here!"

The waitress, Amy, leaves her customer mid-order to come over to us. The customer was literally right in the middle of a sentence when Amy walks away. She's making Claudia seem like Waitress of the Year.

"Amy," Claudia says, "we need an

impartial opinion. Is Snugglepuss the shit, or what?"

Amy pushes her black hair away from her face and I gasp. Behind the pierced nose and eyebrow and black lipstick is the pale face of the girl who OD'd and died at a party about six months from now. I heard about it from my old friend Janie. Amy Richards, her name is. She only worked at Plucky's for about a month before she got fired, so I didn't know her super well, but I remember we shared a few smoke breaks together. And then she died. At twenty-three years old.

"Yeah," Amy says to me. "Snugglepuss is the bomb, lady. And have you seen their lead singer? Majorly hot."

"And their drummer," Claudia adds.

"Absolutely," Amy says.

I want to cry. For a moment, I don't even care about getting Claudia to break up with Jed or this stupid date anymore. I want to be able to do *something* to keep this sweet young girl from dying. Can I warn her to beware of Ecstasy laced with other drugs? Will she listen? Probably not. I mean, the girl thinks Snugglepuss, which sounds like pots and pans being clanged together, is "the bomb." She's not going to listen to a word I say.

"Okay," I finally say. "Maybe you guys are right."

Amy rolls her eyes. "Of course we're right.

Duh. What do you listen to anyway? The Beach Boys?"

Okay, maybe Amy isn't sweet. But it's still really sad this happens to her. I mean, she's kind of a bitch now, but maybe if she'd lived, she'd have gotten her act together, gone back to school, met a nice guy. I'm just sad that she's never going to have that chance, like I did.

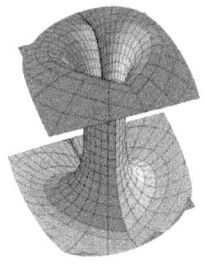

Twelve

Despite the fact that both Claudia and Jed have their own apartments, when I get back to my parents' after having dinner at a restaurant that was *not* shut down by the health inspector, I find the two of them practically having sex on the living room couch. I'm a little irritated, but I can't entirely blame them. My roommate when I was twenty-two was this Russian girl who spoke no English and had horrible BO, and Jed lived above *and* below crack dealers. At the time, I remember being pissed off that my parents wouldn't give me money for a swanky place in Manhattan, but I realize now that having to pay my own way was part of what motivated me to go back to school.

"Hi, Beth," Claudia says as she

disentangles herself from Jed's tentacles. I assume she's on her dinner break, or else she just randomly left her shift midway through, which is also entirely possible.

"Hey," I mumble.

I have to admit, watching them makes me miss Adam. My Adam, that is, not twenty-four-year-old Adam, who hates my guts. I've had a stressful day and it would be nice to lie in his arms. A backrub ... that would be amazing right now. The thought of it almost makes me want to burst into tears.

Because I have nothing better to do, I go into the guest bedroom and I take a nap. My sleeping schedule is still all out of whack. It's like some crazy form of jet lag. Time-travel lag.

When I wake up, I can hear the TV going in the living room. I wander out there, hoping to find Claudia so we can have a little heart-to-heart about why she needs to dump her no-good, (future) cheating boyfriend. But instead, sitting on the couch is her no-good, cheating boyfriend himself. All alone, eating popcorn from a large bowl.

"Why are you here?" I ask him, trying to keep the hostility out of my voice. It's hard because I really hate him.

"It's a good TV," Jed says through bites of popcorn. On the TV screen, Jerry Seinfeld makes a comment about shrinkage and the studio audience laughs. (FYI, women definitely know about shrinkage.)

"Where's Claudia?"

"Went back to work. We're meeting when her shift ends tonight at eleven."

I groan inwardly. It's only eight o'clock now. I want this guy out of my house. He has no right to be hanging out here, spilling popcorn all over the couch and the floor. He's such a selfish asshole. Why can't Claudia see that? It's so obvious. He's an awful boyfriend, yet I can't get her to break up with him.

Jed scratches his balls and I look away. He's really disgusting.

And shallow. He never would have dated me if I weren't so hot back then.

This, of course, gives me an idea. Claudia won't break up with Jed, that much is becoming obvious. But maybe I can talk Jed into ending the relationship. It seems like he could be convinced, if I say the right things.

"I'm kind of hungry," I say. "You feel like going to grab a slice of pizza?"

"Nah, I already kind of ate," Jed says. "Plus I'm comfortable here." To illustrate his point, he scratches his balls again.

All right, obviously I'm not using the right tactic here. How can I lure Jed out of the house? Unfortunately, the answer is obvious. "I thought we could go to Lace," I say.

Jed starts choking on a kernel of popcorn. He looks up at me with watery eyes. "You mean the strip club?"

I force a smile. "You can't visit New York without seeing a strip club, right? You interested?"

He is. Very interested.

***

The whole taxi ride to Lace, Jed can't stop talking about how cool I am. He's been to strip clubs before (of course), but he never met a woman before who was willing to go to one. Claudia *definitely* wouldn't go to a strip club. Did he mention how cool I was?

I'm beginning to get the sense that Jed likes strip clubs. Surprise, surprise.

I have, unfortunately, been to strip clubs before, but I've never been to Lace. It's small and has this intimate feel, which seems like a perfect place to have a talk with Jed about his relationship and why it isn't working. Maybe I can even get him to let Claudia down easy.

We get a table in the back, and I order some chicken wings with a vodka and tonic. I figure if there's a big plate of greasy chicken on our table, no strippers will bother us. Jed immediately becomes mesmerized by the girl dancing on the pole, and I wonder if maybe I didn't make a mistake by bringing him here. He's a little too distracted to have a serious conversation. But at the same time, he's thinking about other women, which is a good thing.

"So how are things going with you and Claudia?" I ask him.

"Oh, you know," he mumbles, not taking his eyes off the stripper.

"That good, huh?" I say.

Jed glances over at me. "Claudia's great," he says. He actually sounds like he means it. "I like her a lot."

Then why did you cheat on me, you dickhead?

"She's got a lot of issues though," I say.

"I thought you just met her yesterday?"

He's slightly smarter than he looks. "Right. And already, I can tell."

Jed frowns at me. I've finally got his attention. "Like what?"

You don't get to be thirty-six years old without learning what sorts of things scare off a guy. "Like, she's obsessed with getting married," I say.

Jed's eyes widen. "She is? She never said anything about that to me."

"Well, of course she wouldn't say it to you," I say, shrugging. "But she's hoping to get married before she turns twenty-three. And have babies, of course. She's really into babies."

Jed nearly spits his beer in my face. "Babies?"

"You don't think babies are cute?" I ask, blinking innocently. "Well, in that case, if I were you, I'd check all your condoms. For holes she poked in them."

Jed is gaping at me now. I can just see the wheels turning in his little brain. "That ... I mean, I don't think Claudia would do that ..."

"Sophia, John, and Rebecca," I say.

Jed shakes his head. "What? Who are they?"

"Your children," I say, like he's stupid not to know. "Those are the names she picked out for them."

How did I come up with those names so fast? Because those are the names I've fantasized about giving to my children someday. But that's not going to happen if I can't get rid of Jed. Luckily, I can tell my idea is working.

"Holy shit ..." Jed leans forward and rubs his temples with his fingers. Poor Claudia. I know for a fact that at age twenty-two, marriage and kids were the last thing on her mind. I just assumed those things would fall into place for me. How wrong I was. Who could have known that I'd have to freaking time travel in order to get my boyfriend to marry me?

Jed is now staring forward, looking a little dazed. I feel kind of bad. I mean, the guy really liked me and now I talked him out of it. But this had to happen.

A black-haired stripper who looks vaguely familiar walks over to our table and runs her hand along Jed's broad shoulder. He gives her a half-hearted smile as I struggle to place her. "Hi, handsome," she says. "Would you like a lap dance?"

"I don't know if I'm in the mood," Jed mumbles. When a man refuses a lap dance, you know he's really upset. Hard to believe.

"Go for it," I say, hoping to seal the deal and get him to break up with Claudia for good. "My treat."

I hand the stripper a bunch of bills and she sits down on an unenthusiastic Jed's lap. "What's your name, handsome?" she asks him.

"I'm Jed," he says.

"Nice to meet you, Jed," she says. "I'm Crystal-Joy."

Now it's my turn to nearly spit out my drink. Crystal-Joy. The stripper that Jed cheated on me with. I still remember her name and how I caught him in bed with her in his apartment, but I forgot when it happened. But now I remember clear as day: it was the end of December, a few days before New Year's Eve. I was so depressed about having no one to kiss when the ball dropped.

Jed just met the stripper he's going to

cheat on me with. And I brought him here. And paid for the freaking lap dance.

I watch the whole thing with some degree of horror. Jed getting more and more into the lap dance. The second lap dance. The third. Lots of alcohol. Crystal-Joy telling him how her shift is over and maybe they could get the hell out of here together. Jed nodding, telling me I should make up an excuse for Claudia.

I could make up all the excuses I want. I could go over to Plucky's and forcibly pin Claudia to the wall and not let her leave. But I've got this terrible feeling that no matter what I do, Claudia is going to walk in on Jed and Crystal-Joy. And all the while, Adam's voice echoes in my ears:

Maybe you can't change the outcome. Maybe the future is unchangeable.

God, I hope not.

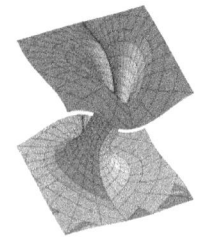

Thirteen

Claudia spends most of the next day crying. I play the part of the good cousin, holding her hand and bringing her a pint of her favorite ice cream (Rocky Road). I feel sorry for Claudia, but more importantly, I'm frustrated that I couldn't stop the whole thing from happening. I was *right there*. It seemed like I should have been able to stop it, yet it was destined to happen just as surely as that taxi slamming into Adam.

"He was the love of my life," Claudia sniffles as she sinks into the couch and takes a bite of Rocky Road. "I'll never love again."

Oh, please. "Come on, Claudia," I say. "He wasn't that great."

"Yes, he was."

"Obviously he wasn't," I say. "He cheated on you."

That didn't help. A fresh wave of tears falls from Claudia's eyes and her nose bubbles over with snot. I'm not attractive when I'm crying. But at twenty-two, you recover quickly from a bout tears—an hour after the waterworks stop, Claudia will look great again. Whereas when I cry, my eyes stay puffy for practically a week.

"You need to forget about that asshole," I say to her.

She wipes her eyes with the back of her hand. "How?"

"A new guy, obviously," I say. "You don't want to spend New Year's pining over Jed, having no one to kiss. Find some new guy and you'll forget all about him."

"I don't know," Claudia mumbles, snuffling loudly.

I take a deep breath. Here's the moment. "I know someone perfect, actually."

Claudia's puffy eyes widen. "Really? Who?"

"His name is Adam," I say. "He's got a great job—he's a computer programmer. And he's really, really cute. He's, um, the son of some friends of my parents."

At the mention of how cute Adam is, Claudia perks up a little. "Do you have a photo?"

Was I really that shallow? "He might be on Facebook."

Claudia frowns. "Whose facebook?"

Oh, right. It's 1999 and there's no Facebook yet. Hmm, maybe I should tip Adam off and get him to invent Facebook. Of course, he's already rich. He doesn't need to invent Facebook.

"Never mind," I say. "He's cute. Trust me."

Claudia takes another thoughtful bite of Rocky Road. "All right," she says. "I'll go out with him. But it's got to be December 30. I don't want to waste New Year's on him if it turns out he sucks."

I give myself a little pat on the back. I got Claudia to agree to a date with Adam! Okay, she doesn't know about the whole wheelchair deal, but that's a necessity. If she knows, she won't go on the date, but I'm sure once she sees him, she'll fall instantly in love and she won't care. I mean, that's what happened when I met Adam in 2012.

While Claudia is taking a nap (I guess I took naps when I was twenty-two), I find the napkin with Adam's phone number and give him a call. I'm relieved when he picks up right away. "Hi, Adam," I say. "It's Beth. The Psychic Girl."

"Hey, Beth," he says. His voice hasn't changed at all in the last fourteen years and the sound of him makes me incredibly homesick. I want to reach through the phone and give him a hug. "What's up?"

"So that girl Claudia?" I remind him. "She wants to have dinner on December 30th. Are you free?"

"That's Thursday, right?" he says. "Yeah, sure, I can do it."

"Great," I say, breathing a sigh of relief.

"Where does she want to go?"

I think for minute, trying to remember which restaurants were around fourteen years ago. "Do you know that middle eastern restaurant, Mediterranean?"

"Yeah, I know it. It's got four steps to enter. Try again."

"Oh," I say. You'd think after dating Adam for a year, I'd be more on the ball about stuff like that. "How about Angelo's on 38th Street?"

He thinks for a second. "Yeah, that sounds fine. Is seven o'clock okay?"

"Yes, perfect."

There's silence between us. I don't want to hang up. I miss him. I want to tell him how much I miss him, how much I love him, but that would be weird, obviously. He barely knows who I am.

"So, um," he says. "Is there anything I should, like, bring her?"

"What do you mean?"

"Like, you know, does she like flowers?"

I think for a second, trying to remember what would have impressed me when I was twenty-two. "You can get her a single red rose."

"A rose, got it," he says. He's quiet for a minute, then he says, kind of sheepishly, "Thanks for doing this, Beth. You were right about needing to get out there again."

"I think you two will really hit it off," I say confidently.

"And she really doesn't mind that I'm … you know, that I use a wheelchair?"

She absolutely doesn't mind. Because she doesn't know. "She's definitely going to like you, Adam," I assure him. "Don't worry."

"Right," he says, and then he laughs nervously. "I'm a *little* worried."

"Don't be," I say. "I know Claudia really well, and I know you two are perfect for each other."

"Okay," he says. "I believe you."

Of course, there's a small part of me that worries maybe twenty-two-year-old Claudia is not perfect for twenty-four-year-old Adam. I've changed a lot in the last fourteen years, and maybe the person I was back then wasn't ready for the kind of great guy Adam is. But I can't think that way. I have to believe in myself (my former self). Claudia will fall in love in two days and the rest will be history. Or the future. Whatever.

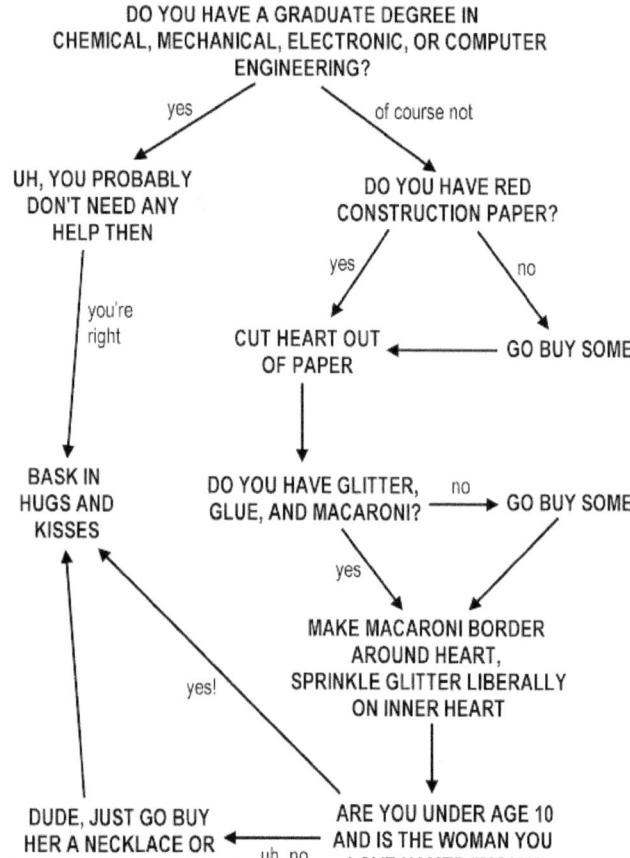

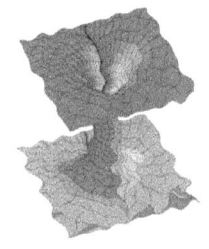

Fourteen

Claudia is really excited about her date with Adam, to the point where she spends the entire next day shopping for clothes with money I know she doesn't have. She's a waitress, after all. And Plucky's was not exactly a high-end restaurant. I used to sometimes get extra work doing commercials and that paid really well, but those jobs tended to be few and far between. My life was so aimless back then.

My minor victory is that I manage to convince Claudia to take it easy on the eye make-up for her date with Adam. "You're so naturally pretty," I say. "You really don't need so much make-up."

"Thanks, Beth," she says. "I hope I'm as

pretty as you when I'm your age."

Seriously, sometimes I'm not sure whether I want to hug her or slap her. She's trying, at least.

She looks really good in a floral-print skirt that falls just above her knees and a low cut maroon blouse. Ordinarily, I would have shared with her my advice about not shaving her legs prior to the date in order to ensure she'll remain chaste, but I'm not so worried about Adam. I know he'll be a gentleman.

As Claudia tugs on her coat, she starts to look a little nervous. "I've never been on a blind date before," she says. "Do you think you could come with me?"

I stare at her. "Come with you on your date?"

Claudia laughs. "No, I mean, just … come to the restaurant. Point him out and introduce us."

Actually, that's not a terrible idea. It will ensure that Claudia doesn't make a run for it when she sees Adam. "Okay."

Even though it's not very far to the restaurant, Claudia insists we grab a cab because she doesn't want to mess up her hair. In the taxi, she keeps crossing and uncrossing her legs, and it takes me a minute to realize I'm doing the exact same thing. I had no idea that was a nervous habit of mine. I make a conscious effort to stop.

When we get to Angelo's, Claudia quickly whips out her compact and takes a last minute look at herself. She nods to herself and then smiles brightly at me. "Let's go," she says.

We get into the restaurant, which is pretty large and fairly busy, and we tell the hostess we're meeting someone here. I immediately spot Adam near the front. He's wearing a really nice light blue dress shirt that's actually buttoned correctly, a dark tie, and he's made an effort to tame his short brown hair. He's yanking at his tie, looking about as freaked out as I feel.

"So where is he?" Claudia whispers in my ear.

"Over there," I say, pointing in Adam's direction.

Claudia cranes her neck. "Where? Behind the guy in the wheelchair?"

Oh, no. I've got a bad feeling about this. "No," I say. "That's him. In the wheelchair."

Claudia stares at me then grips my forearm hard enough to leave finger imprints behind. "Are you fucking *kidding* me? You set me up with a cripple?"

You wouldn't think the situation could get any worse, but at that moment, Adam spots us and waves enthusiastically. I want to cry. "I told you," I say. "He's really nice. And he's cute, don't you think?"

Claudia is shaking her head at me. "No. I

just … *no.*"

"Listen to me," I say. I want to give her a shake. "You can*not* stand him up. He's *right there.* He's a great guy and he won't ever cheat on you with a stripper."

"Well, duh," Claudia says. "A stripper probably wouldn't even sleep with him."

I glance over at Adam, who is now looking at us curiously. I wonder if he's figured out that Claudia is having second thoughts.

"Okay, fine," Claudia says through her teeth. "I'll have dinner with him. But that's it, Beth. No more dates."

I have to hold onto Claudia's arm and actually physically drag her over to Adam's table. She's really demonstrating passive resistance here. When we get to the table, she's scowling. I try to make up for it by being extra enthusiastic. "Hi, Adam!" I say. "I'd like you to meet my cousin, Claudia Williams. Claudia, this is Adam Schaffer."

"Hi, Claudia," Adam says.

"Hi," Claudia mumbles, not sitting down.

Adam pulls the rose out from under the table. "I got this for you."

Claudia takes it from him as if he just handed her a wet, snotty napkin. "Thank you."

The three of us all stare at each other in silence. This is not going super great. "So I should probably go," I say.

Claudia grabs my arm. "No, Beth, don't go. Join us."

She's really got a death grip on my arm. I had no idea I used to be so strong. "I really shouldn't ..."

"Beth doesn't know anyone in town," Claudia says to Adam. "She's just going to be all alone tonight. You wouldn't mind if she joined us, right?"

"Of course not," Adam says. "Please join us, Beth."

They're both looking at me. I can't join Adam and Claudia on their date. How can they fall in love if I'm sitting right here?

"I just ... I can't," I stammer. "There's no chair for me ..."

"Well, that's something we can't possibly fix," Adam says, with an amused expression on his face. He's always been good at calling me on my bullshit.

Sure enough, the waiter is able to dig up another chair for me. Claudia doesn't let go of me until I'm sitting right between her and Adam—she's left behind a set of angry red marks on my upper arm from her nails. I try to make peace with this new development, thinking at least if I'm here, I'll be able to help foster romance.

"So what do you do, Claudia?" Adam asks her.

"I'm an actress," Claudia lies. Well, I

suppose it's not entirely a lie. I guess I sort of considered myself an actress when I first returned to New York after college. Mostly I got auditions for small parts in TV shows and commercials, and usually I didn't get the roles. I got told that they wanted someone "more ethnic," so for a brief time, I dyed my hair jet black to look more ethnic. And then I lost the "all-American girl" jobs. I couldn't win, so I eventually gave up.

"Really?" Adam raises his eyebrows. "Would I have seen you in anything?"

"I was in a toothpaste commercial," Claudia says.

"What brand?"

I still remember flashing my pearly whites for that stupid toothpaste commercial, but I can't for the life of me remember what brand it was. I look at Claudia and it's clear she doesn't remember either. "One of the big ones," she says.

Adam nods. "That sounds really fun."

It wasn't. "Oh, yes," Claudia says. "It's definitely fun. Hey, can we get some wine or something to drink?"

"Of course." Adam signals for the waiter. We each order a glass of wine, but Claudia looks like she wants to order two or three glasses. She excuses herself to go to the bathroom, and I'm left alone with Adam, who is looking at me rather accusingly.

"I thought you said she was okay with my situation," Adam says, frowning at me.

"She is," I insist.

"Yeah, right."

"She is!"

The waiter returns with our wine and a basket of bread. Adam picks up his glass and takes a long drink. "Are you capable of doing anything besides lying? Because I've yet to see it."

I take a long swig off my own glass of wine. We should have just told the waiter to leave the whole bottle. "She going to fall totally in love with you," I say. "Trust me."

"You're wrong," Adam says. "Trust me."

"And how do you know?"

"Because she just left."

I whip my head around to look at the back of the restaurant. The front door is swinging slightly with a recent departure. I turn back around and stare at Adam. "She didn't …"

"I assure you, she did."

Damn. I should have gone with her to the bathroom. I should have known I'd try to pull something like this. "I'm sorry," I say miserably.

"So what is this, anyway?" Adam asks me. "Are you just going to, like, appear every two years to wreck my life?"

"I'm sorry," I say again, because what else can I say?

Adam pulls a roll from the basket. He pulls out a packet of butter and starts to butter his roll. "You know what? It's okay."

"It is?"

He shrugs. "Well, I don't love that she ran out on me, but I knew it wasn't going to work out. She's not my type anyway."

Hmph. I beg to differ. "Why not?"

"She kind of seems like a spoiled brat," he says. "And that whole thing about being an actress? Who does she think she's kidding? She's probably a waitress or she works at the Gap or something."

"She's not ... I mean, she doesn't ..." I bite my lip. "Okay, she does wait tables. But she's not a spoiled brat. She's really nice."

He shrugs again. "Whatever you say."

"She is!"

Adam chuckles. "Well, don't take it *personally*, Beth. She's just kind of immature, that's all."

"Immature?"

"I like girls who are a little more ... substantial," he says. "She looks like her biggest priority is what shade of lipstick to put on."

"That's not true," I insist. I also used to care about my nails. And my hair, of course.

But other than that, he's right on the money.

This really sucks. Adam doesn't like

Claudia, and Claudia definitely doesn't like Adam. How are they supposed to fall in love? Then again, maybe this is a good sign. In romantic comedies, don't the two leads always hate each other before they fall desperately in love?

Except right now it doesn't *feel* like a good sign.

"Will you stay, at least?" Adam asks me. "I don't want to look like a loser who had two girls run out on him."

"I'll stay," I promise.

"Good." He takes another sip of wine. "So what do you do, Beth? Aside from being psychic."

"I'm a teacher," I say.

"Yeah?" He has the same impressed look as he did when I told him when I met him at the dinner party. "That's awesome. What grade?"

"First grade."

"Do you like it?"

"I love it," I say. "Six year olds are so … earnest. They don't have any hidden agenda. They're so good and pure."

"It's a great age," Adam agrees. "I have a six-year-old nephew and he's really incredible. He says the funniest things. He told me the other day that I was bionic."

I laugh. "I can definitely see one of my kids saying that."

"So what's your best teacher story?" he asks.

"There are way too many to choose from," I say thoughtfully. "I can tell you one that happened recently, though."

"Go for it."

"So this girl in my class named Madison raises her hand—"

Adam snorts. "Madison? That's the name of a girl? Isn't that, like, the name of a president? Who the hell calls their kid Madison?"

I bite my tongue to keep from telling him that every third girl is named Madison in 2013. "*Anyway*, Madison raises her hand and asks me in front of the whole class if Santa Claus is real."

"Uh oh! What did you say?"

"I wasn't sure," I admit. "I asked her what she thought. She told me she thought Santa might be her parents and her grandparents." I smile. "Then, just as I was freaking out that she was going to spoil it for everyone, she adds, 'Either Santa is my parents or he's a magical man who just comes to life during Christmas and makes presents for every kid in the world.'"

"Whew," Adam says. "Close call."

"No kidding."

"Would you get fired if you told the kids that Santa wasn't real?"

"I might. Parents are pretty sensitive about that. You know, keeping the magic alive."

"You mean, lying to their kids," he says, grinning at me.

"Well, yeah," I admit. "I mean, it's lying, but I think a lie can be justified if you're doing it to create some magic for your kid. My parents were never about the magic. They told me straight out that they were buying the presents for me. I mean, I got some pretty great presents, but I would have traded it for a little magic, you know? How about you?"

"Oh, my parents were all about the magic," Adam says. "When I was six, I firmly believed in Santa and not even a sexy teacher could have convinced me otherwise."

I ignore his comment about the "sexy teacher" and say, "I bet you were an adorable six-year-old."

"Well, yeah," Adam says, shrugging. "What six-year-old isn't adorable? I wasn't like some mutant kid."

I laugh again. I study Adam's young face, and realize that no matter how much he looks like my boyfriend, he's not. Not exactly, anyway. Which means I can say things to him that I can't say to Adam in 2013 because I don't need to worry about scaring him off. If I ask him his ideas about relationships, it won't sound like I'm pressuring him. "Do you want kids?"

"I do," he says. "Just got to meet the girl, you know?"

I feel a touch of bitterness. I want to yell at him that he's *going* to meet the girl, and he's not going to want to marry her. But that would probably just confuse him. I can't very well scold him for something he hasn't done yet.

Adam's eyes flit down at my left hand. "Are you married?"

I shake my head. "No, never."

"Are you in a relationship?" he asks.

I hesitate. I don't think I've ever been asked such a complicated question. "Sort of. He's … very far away right now."

"He's an idiot then," Adam says, his eyes on my face.

The way he's looking at me is making me kind of breathless. This is kind of weird. Adam is supposed to be falling in love with my twenty-two-year-old self. That's why I came here in the first place. He's not supposed to be undressing thirty-six-year-old me with his eyes. I'm old enough to be his mother. (I am! There are twelve-year-olds who are capable of having kids.)

The tension is broken when the waiter comes to take our orders. I take an extra-long time ordering my food, hoping that the moment will be completely ended and Adam will stop looking at me that way. We need to get back on track here.

"So what do you do?" I ask him, trying to steer the conversation away from anything romantic.

"Don't you know?" he asks. "Aren't you psychic?"

"You're a computer programmer," I say.

He nods, not looking at all surprised that I know.

"And in your free time, you invent stuff," I add.

Adam looks at me and laughs. "I do? Wow, you have to work on your psychic skills, lady. Who do you think I am—Thomas Edison?"

"So you don't invent stuff?" I ask. I had assumed that was something Adam always did, but I guess that must have started later.

"No, that would be *really* nerdy," he says. "Like, over the top. It's not like I don't already have trouble meeting women."

"I wish you'd give Claudia another chance," I can't help but say.

Adam is quiet for a minute, then he says, "I don't want to talk about Claudia anymore, okay?"

The truth is, I don't want to talk about her, either.

***

Adam and I have a really good time at dinner. I love thirty-eight-year-old Adam, but I really like twenty-four-year-old Adam. He's sweet, he's funny, and he's smart. I keep thinking to myself that I wish I had met him when I was younger, then I realize that I *did* meet him when I was younger. And I snuck out of the restaurant.

When the check comes, I try to reach for it, but Adam is much too quick for me. He snatches it up with lightning speed. "You should let me pay," I say. "I was the one who bulldozed you into this terrible dinner."

"Not a chance in hell," he says.

So I let him pay, although I'm worried about going down some slippery slope here. He needs to recognize that I am way too old for him and our relationship can't be anything but platonic. At least for another fourteen years.

"So, I was thinking," Adam says. "Claudia told me you don't know many people in the city. Is that true?"

"Yes ..."

"Great," he says. "Would you like to keep me company tomorrow night for New Year's? We can watch the ball drop on TV."

My stomach turns to butterflies. "Don't you have a party to go to?"

Adam shrugs. "Nothing I really feel like going to, you know?"

I spent last New Year's with Adam. We went out to dinner with some friends, then came back to his house, where we kissed at midnight. 2013 felt like such a perfect new year. I was certain that I'd met the love of my life and we were going to be together forever. Now … I'm not certain of anything anymore.

"Okay," I say.

"Yeah?" Adam's eyes light up. "That's great. How about ten o'clock?"

"Sounds good," I nod. I remember the address Adam wrote down for me the first time I time traveled. "Apartment 14F, right?"

Adam gives me a sideways look. "Eventually are you going to tell me how you know so much about me?"

"Of course," I say vaguely.

He doesn't look like he entirely believes me, rightfully so, but then he gets distracted when he notices that the red rose he brought for Claudia is still lying on the table. He picks it up and twirls it between his thumb and his forefinger. "I guess your cousin isn't into roses, huh?"

"I guess not," I mumble. It's nicer than saying that she *is* into roses—she's just not into him. "Hey, you should be careful. You're going to cut your hand on a thorn."

Adam grins crookedly. "Not with these callouses I'm not." He holds out his palms for me to examine, but I'm not impressed. These callouses are nothing compared to what he'll have fourteen years from now, but I can't very well say that.

"You may as well take it," he says, holding the rose out to me.

Against my better judgment, I reach for the flower. For just a second, my fingers brush against his ever so slightly. I've touched Adam's bare skin thousands of times in the past (well, the future), which is why I'm so surprised by the tingling that shoots through my entire arm. I can feel my cheeks starting to turn red as the rose, and I lower my eyes, hoping he doesn't notice. Even though he'd have to be blind not to.

"I'll give it to Claudia," I mumble, even though I have no intention of doing any such thing.

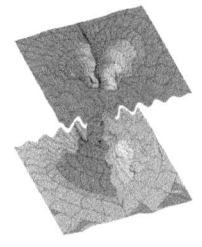

Fifteen

I still remember when I first fell in love with Adam in 2012.

When we had been dating about four months, his father died. Adam is the youngest of his siblings, so his father was at least seventy, but it was still very sudden. Apparently, the elderly Mr. Schaffer was walking out to the mailbox to pick up their daily mail and dropped dead of a massive heart attack. By the time Adam's mother found him out there, it was too late to even call an ambulance, but she did anyway and the EMTs pronounced him dead at the scene.

It's interesting, I guess, that it never seemed to occur to Adam to use his time machine to try to save his dad's life. Then again, it sounded like Mr. Schaffer had already been told by every member of his family to go see a doctor. Going back in time wasn't going to fix the clogged arteries in his father's heart.

The night he died, Adam and I were supposed to see a movie together. *The Avengers*. I heard the phone ringing while I was in the shower, and I made a naked run for it, dripping water all over the carpeting of my studio, screaming, "Wait! Wait!" I saw Adam's name on my phone and smiled instinctively, picking up the line seconds before it went to voicemail. "Hey," I said breathlessly. "What's going on?"

"I can't make it tonight," he said. I felt that twinge of annoyance that I get when someone cancels plans on me at the last minute. Adam always seemed much too considerate to pull a move like that. Then he added, "My dad died."

"Adam," I gasped. "I'm so sorry."

"Yeah," he said and I heard him swallow. He wasn't crying but he sounded miserable. "I'm going to see if I could get a flight to Cleveland tonight."

"Can I come?" I asked.

"You want to come?" Adam sounded surprised but not particularly displeased.

"Well, my dinner plans cancelled," I said. Then I felt bad for making a joke at a time like this.

"I'll see if I can get two tickets," Adam

said. Then he added, "Thanks, Claudia."

He managed to get a flight out of LaGuardia and met me at my apartment in a taxi. When I climbed into the taxi, I inspected Adam's face for swollen eyes or a red nose and I didn't see it. He looked fairly composed, considering everything. I tried to remember Adam ever saying much about his dad, and I couldn't. I hadn't even met his parents yet.

"Were you close to your dad?" I asked him when we got on the FDR drive. The cabbie was driving like a maniac and I was holding onto the seat for dear life.

"Not recently, I guess," he said. "He was kind of pissed off when I went to NYU instead of going to Ohio State or something like that. He thinks New York is a waste. He wanted me to come home after my injury, like, permanently, but I just hated the idea of moving back in with my parents. On top of everything else, it would have been so depressing."

"He must be proud of you, though."

Adam frowned at me. "Proud of what?"

"Well, because you're a good guy," I say.

Adam just shook his head. Apparently, in his head, that wasn't worth his father being proud of him for. Although I think it ought to be.

When we got to the airport, I learned about some of the realities of traveling with a wheelchair. At the security check-in, the guards had to frisk Adam then do a search of his wheelchair as well. I was worried they were going to make him check his wheelchair with the bags, but they let him hang onto it till we got to the gate and were getting close to boarding.

At the gate of the place, I got introduced to the "aisle chair" — an extra-narrow wheelchair that would fit down the aisle in the plane. A steward brought it out to him and offered him help getting into it, which he refused since he was able to make the transfer on his own. A seatbelt went across Adam's chest like an X. "Do you want us to secure your legs?" they asked him as his legs flopped out of the confines of the narrow chair. He nodded and a second belt was secured just below his knees.

"I hate this part," Adam confided in me as he rescued his seat cushion off his wheelchair just before they hauled it off.

The good news was that we were allowed to get on the plane ahead of everyone else. The one bonus on top of all the hassle. When I pointed that out to him, he said, "Yeah, but it means we get off last."

By the time we arrived in Ohio, we were both exhausted and not looking forward to the hassle of picking up the rental car and then driving to our hotel in Akron. And we definitely weren't ready for the revelation that Adam's wheelchair had been accidentally sent to Chicago.

"You're kidding me," he said, staring at the apologetic stewardess.

"I'm so sorry," she said. "But we can get it back by tomorrow morning. In the meantime, do you need a loaner?"

"Yes," he said tightly. "I do."

I wouldn't have blamed Adam if he had burst into tears right then and there, but he obligingly climbed into the bulky, hospital-grade wheelchair they brought him. Like the aisle chair, it had large handles in the back, and instead of his single footplate, there were two awkwardly connected footrests that were at different heights.

As if things couldn't get any worse, when we got to the rental car place, they told us that they had a great Ford Focus waiting for us. "With hand controls," Adam clarified.

"Oh, I'm so sorry about that," the rental car lady said. "We couldn't get that on such short notice. Can you manage?"

Adam looked up at me and I nodded. "Sure, I can drive."

Let me tell you something about girls from Manhattan: we're not great drivers. The public transportation system in the city is so amazing, there was no reason to get behind the wheel until I was eighteen years old. They don't even *offer* driving tests in Manhattan—I had to go out to Brooklyn to take the test, and it took me five tries to pass it, and only then because I got a very sympathetic male examiner. (Seriously, it was the worst parking job in the history of the world. We had to hail a taxi to get back to the curb.) But I have my license, I understand which one is the gas pedal and which is the brake—it's not rocket science, for God's sake. It's easier than inventing a time machine.

So I got behind the wheel of the Ford and followed the GPS directions to the hotel. By about halfway through our journey to the hotel, Adam was hanging on to the dashboard and staring at me in terror. I thought it was a little bit of an overreaction.

When we got to the hotel, we were completely exhausted and absolutely ready to just crash (not literally, although just barely). We got to the reception desk, and Adam told the clerk his name, and she gave him the keys to room 203. "Thanks," he said. "Where's the elevator?"

"There's no elevator," the clerk said, as if it was completely ridiculous to expect something like that.

Adam looked over at the long flight of stairs to get to the second floor. He shook his head and turned back to the clerk. "Can you please give us a room on the first floor, then?"

"I'm so sorry," she said. "There's a big wedding this weekend, and we're completely booked."

Adam stared up at the clerk in disbelief. "I told you on the phone that I needed accommodations and you said it was fine. How am I supposed to get up there?"

She flashed him a toothy smile. "I'm so sorry, sir. We can definitely accommodate you by storing your wheelchair for you during your visit."

Adam just shook his head again and canceled our reservation.

We called every hotel in the area and everything was booked up with the stupid wedding. I suggested expanding to a larger radius, but Adam was too scared of me getting back on the highway. Finally, he sighed and said, "Let's just go to my parents' house."

I hated the fact that I had to meet Adam's mother under these circumstances. She greeted us at the back door to her two-story house with the puffy eyes that Adam was lacking. Her gray hair was completely disheveled, and she was clutching her robe together with her fist. "I'm so glad to meet you, Claudia," she said in a strained voice. I could tell she was trying to be nice, but she just didn't have it in her right then.

She made up the den for us, which had a fold-out couch. As she led us to the room, she said to me, "Claudia, do you want to sleep in my sewing room?"

"It's okay, Mom," Adam said quickly.

"Claudia will stay with me."

I felt a little embarrassed, but then again, Adam was thirty-seven and I was thirty-five. Pretending like we were virgin teenagers would have been a little ridiculous. Of course, my parents still act like I haven't had sex yet, that I'm saving myself for marriage. As if.

The fold-out couch was surprisingly comfortable. We were both so tired and the second my head hit the pillow and I snuggled up in the down comforter, I was down for the count.

I thought Adam was as tired as I was, but I woke up at about two a.m., and saw him in the moonlight, clearly wide awake. As my eyes adjusted to the light, I could see tears running down his cheeks. I reached out and put my hand on his chest. "Adam?"

He wiped his eyes with the back of his hand. "I'm sorry," he managed. "I didn't mean to wake you."

"Are you okay?" I asked. Stupid question. I mean, his father just died.

"This has just been the worst day ever," he said as a fresh wave of tears spilled from his eyes. He took a few deep breaths, trying to get himself under control. "They lost my fucking wheelchair, we couldn't get a car or a hotel room that I could use ... and ... and my dad died."

This time he didn't even try to hold back the tears. He sobbed into my oversized T-shirt, soaking the sleeve with saltwater. I held him, just letting him have this release. I'd never seen him lose control of himself this way before. Well, except during sexy time.

"I'm really glad you're here with me," he whispered to me, after the tears had mostly subsided.

"I'm glad I'm here too."

He looked at me and I could see even in the dark that his eyes were bloodshot. "I love you, Claudia."

Truthfully, I had known he felt that way for a while. A girl can tell. I didn't feel the same way, and I was relieved that he knew better than to say it to me. But at this moment, I realized that for the first time, I *did* feel the same way. I loved him and I wanted him to know it.

"I love you, too," I said.

***

Claudia doesn't seem the least bit sorry about running out on the date last night. I catch her curled up on the couch in a tank top and underwear, eating the leftover Rocky Road ice cream when I get home. She's watching *Sex and the City* on television, and she doesn't even acknowledge what she did to me. "I don't get this show," Claudia says. "Carrie isn't even pretty. Why do all these guys like her?"

"I don't get it either," I say.

"If I were thirty-four and single, I would just get married," Claudia says, as if it's just that simple.

"I always thought Carrie should have married Aidan," I say.

Claudia looks up at me. "Who?"

Oh, right. *Sex and the City* has only been on a year or two. Carrie Bradshaw hasn't met Aidan Shaw yet. "Never mind," I say.

Claudia shoves a spoonful of ice cream into her mouth. "So are you going to scream at me for ditching you?"

"No," I say, "but it was a pretty shitty thing to do."

"You deserved it," she says. "You should have told me he was disabled. How could you not tell me that?"

"I didn't want you to be prejudiced against him before you even met him."

Claudia rolls her eyes. "Look, I'm sure he's a real nice guy, but I am just not interested in dating someone like that. Nobody is."

"*Nobody* is?"

"Nobody normal, anyway," she says.

Was I really like this when I was twenty-two? Was my mind seriously that closed?

In any case, I know it's a lost cause to invite Claudia to Adam's apartment tomorrow night. Even if I managed to trick her into going,

I'd have to hogtie her to get her to stay. She has zero interest in Adam. My plan, the whole reason I came back to 1999, is a complete and utter failure.

Which means I need a new plan.

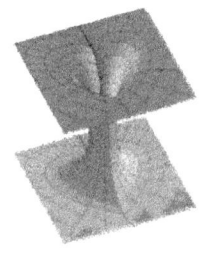

Sixteen

I show up at Adam's apartment the next day carrying a six-pack of Coronas. I've always been taught it's good to be fashionably late, so I show up at ten fifteen p.m. Even though it means that I sit outside on the steps of the brownstone next to his building for twenty minutes before it's fashionable to go inside. Then I just feel like an idiot.

When Adam opens the door, I see he's dressed casually in jeans and a dark green T-shirt. He wheels back to let me enter and his eyes light up when he sees the six-pack. "You really are psychic," he says. "I thought I was going to have to make a beer run."

I grab two of the beers for us, then he

wheels over to his fridge to store the rest inside. I stroll around his apartment, getting a twinge of déjà vu because it looks so much like his current set-up. It's different furniture (thank God), but there's a certain style to it all—a certain *Adamness*. Everything is old to the point of nearly falling apart, but at the same time looks incredibly comfortable. His couch is even ripped in all the same places his couch is ripped in 2013.

I sink down into the couch and can't help but notice all the rings on his coffee table. He's got a bowl of chips on the table and some guacamole and salsa set up. I dip one of the chips into the guacamole—it's really good. The salsa looks a little questionable though. "Did you make these?" I ask him.

Adam calls out to me from the kitchen: "Guacamole, yes. Salsa, no."

Adam wheels back into the living room, then transfers out of his wheelchair to sit next to me on the couch. He's not right next to me, but then again, it's not a very large couch. We're pretty close. I debate if I should edge away from him, but I don't want to insult him. It's not like he has cooties or anything.

Adam grabs the remote and tunes in to Dick Clark hosting the New Year's Eve festivities. I can hear Prince's "1999" playing in the background. "I am so sick of that song," Adam says.

"Yeah, no kidding," I laugh.

"Now I just want you to know," he says, "that just in case some apocalypse hits at midnight, I've got the place stocked with plenty of canned goods."

I frown at him. "What are you talking about?"

"You know," he says, grinning at me. "Y2K. World might end. Computers will take over. Something like that."

"Oh, right," I say. I forgot all about Y2K. It seemed like such a big deal at the time. "Nothing's going to happen at midnight. We'll never hear about this stupid Y2K thing again."

"Well, that's a relief coming from you, Psychic Girl."

I blush. "I told you, I'm not actually psychic."

"Is that so?" Adam raises his eyebrows. "Well then, how would you like to explain all the things you know about me?"

I just stare at him. No believable lies are coming to mind.

"Feeling a little more psychic now, huh?" he says.

"Guess so."

We watch the bands play at Times Square. I have to say, you know you're getting old when the thought of being out in Times Square to see the ball drop makes you feel physically ill. I mean, it's freezing out there, everybody is packed into a tiny little space, and you feel like there's barely room to breathe, even though you're outdoors. Plus it just seems exhausting.

I remember enjoying it when I did it though. I'd always be with some guy, we'd be sharing a smoke, and he'd be keeping me warm with his body heat. Everyone around us would be drunk, including myself, and we would all just be so happy and excited.

Adam, as if reading my mind (for a change), says, "You ever been to Times Square for New Year's?"

"I went a few times," I recall. "It was fun at the time, but it's not an experience I'm eager to repeat."

"I went about four years ago," he says. He looks over at his wheelchair. "I don't think I could manage it anymore. Anyway, I'm too old."

"Too old?" I snort. "You're only twenty-four!"

"Scarily accurate guess, as usual, Psychic Girl," Adam notes, studying my face. Damn, he's got me again. "Right, I'm twenty-four. Which I think is too old to *schlep* out to Times Square to see the ball drop."

"Whatever," I say. "*I'm* too old to go to Times Square. *You're* definitely not too old."

"Yeah, you're ancient," he says sarcastically. "What are you—twenty-eight?

Twenty-nine?"

Ha. I am starting to love this guy. It's especially nice to hear after Claudia treated me like I was the World's Oldest Woman. "A little older," I admit. I don't need to lie about my age with him, but I'm kind of grateful when he doesn't make any more guesses.

We continue to watch TV and make small talk until it gets close to midnight. We finish our beers then I run to get us each a second beer from the fridge. I start to get a nice buzz going, and Adam's face gets that glow he always has when he's been drinking. I'm sure the alcohol has something to do with this, but it's weird how there isn't a trace of awkwardness between us. Even though this isn't my Adam, he's just as easy to talk to as the 2013 version of himself.

And he's just as good at making me laugh. Although with two beers in me, I'm an easy target.

Adam's got a bottle of wine and some nice glasses sitting on the end table, so he grabs them when we're at the five-minute mark. "You like Merlot, I hope?" he asks, jimmying out the cork with his thumbs.

"Love it," I say.

He pours the wine into glasses and hands me mine. We clink glasses and Adam says, "Cheers."

I take a sip. It's really good. It tastes

expensive, but I'm afraid to ask how much he paid. "Got any New Year's resolutions?"

Adam is eying me. "Yeah. One."

I'm about to ask what exactly he means by that when the countdown starts till the ball drops. We both watch the screen intently as the shimmering ball makes its way down the pole. *Ten ... nine ... eight ... seven ...*

Adam is closer to me than I realized. He gently pulls the wine glass out of my hand.

Six ... five ... four ...

I feel his fingers stroke the underside of my jaw, bringing my face closer to his. I come, almost as if I'm in a trance.

Three ... two ... one ...

And now he's kissing me. His lips are on mine, his hands on my neck, in my hair. It's so oddly familiar, yet different. He's my Adam, but he's not. They say you can only have one first kiss, but here we are. I know this must be somehow wrong, but it feels so good that it's hard to push him away. Our lips don't separate for what feels like fifteen minutes, at least.

"Christ," Adam says breathily. "I've wanted to do that ever since I first saw you two years ago."

"You did?"

"Hell, yeah."

And then he kisses me again, demonstrating just how intensely he wants me. I remember that he hasn't been with a woman, hasn't even kissed a woman, in over two years. How can I refuse him if that's the case? Anyway, if he kisses me, then The Bitch won't be his first, and she won't be able to destroy him the way she did. I can still save him, even if young Claudia won't get within throwing distance of him.

Maybe letting Adam kiss me is the right thing to do. And not just because I want it so badly.

***

The rest of the night is kind of a blur. At some point, Adam gets back into his wheelchair and I climb into his lap so that he can give me a ride to his bed. He's done this a hundred times before in 2013, but I know it's new to him in 1999 (well, 2000 now, I guess). We're both giggling a lot and he keeps stopping to kiss me. I hear him grunt slightly with my extra weight because he isn't as strong as he eventually will be.

We mostly kiss when we're in bed. We lie in bed together, fully dressed, and he kisses me. He's a little bit shy and only goes so far as to put his hand under my shirt and on my bare belly. He has callouses on his hand, but they're not as firm and widespread as they will be in 2013. I bite my lip a few times, longing for the man that he someday will be, but still glad that I at least have part of him right now.

Eventually, we fall asleep together, me tucked under his arm. He sleeps easily without his Ambien. He probably doesn't even have a prescription yet.

I haven't slept well since I left 2013, but tonight I sleep like the dead. When I wake up, I look at the clock and it's nearly noon. I can't even believe I slept that long. I haven't done that since I was ... well, Claudia's age. At age thirty-six, I wake up at seven a.m., even on weekends.

Adam's eyes crack open next to me and he smiles wide when he sees me. "Wow," he says. "I thought for a second it was all just a dream."

"Nope," I say.

He raises his eyebrows at me. "Any regrets?"

"Absolutely not."

"Me either," he says. "But then again, I'm sure I don't have to tell you that."

I reach out and touch his chin, my fingers grazing the scar along his jawline under his five o'clock shadow. He knows what I'm doing and says, almost apologetically, "I broke my jaw."

"I know," I say, before I can stop myself.

"Of course you do, Psychic Girl," he says, rolling his eyes.

He starts to push away my hand, but I won't let him. "It's very sexy," I say.

"Yeah, right."

"It really is," I insist.

He must at least sort of believe me, because he visibly relaxes and allows me to touch his face. I have to build up his self-confidence, make him realize how sexy and desirable he is. That's part of the plan. Hopefully, it's working.

Adam insists on making me breakfast in bed, even though it's more like lunchtime. Which is okay, because breakfast in bed turns out to be sliced turkey sandwiches on white bread. And mayonnaise—way, way too much mayonnaise for a woman on a perpetual diet. He puts two of them on a plate and wheels back into the bedroom, where he puts the plate on the bed. He transfers back into bed next to me, and we eat the sandwiches next to each other in bed, like we're having a picnic. He doesn't even whine about crumbs, which my Adam definitely does when we eat in bed together.

"So what do you want to do today?" he asks me. "Movie?"

"Sure," I say.

"Do you want to see *Man on the Moon*?" he asks. "You know, that movie about Andy Kaufman?"

"Ugh," I groan. "I've seen that movie like five times and I've never liked it. Jim Carrey should have stuck to comedy, seriously."

Adam stares at me. "What are you talking about? That movie came out last week."

Crap. "Oh, sorry. I thought you were talking about *Apollo 13*, that movie about *going* to the moon."

He doesn't look convinced. "But you were talking about Jim Carrey. Jim Carrey wasn't in *Apollo 13*."

Double crap. "Uh, he wasn't?"

We just look at each other for a minute, then Adam finally shakes his head at me. I think he's given up on trying to figure me out. At least, I hope he has.

We finally settle on seeing *The Talented Mr. Ripley*, even though I've actually already seen it twice, but at least Jude Law is hot. Adam hits the showers before I do, and he doesn't undress in front of me, not even a little bit. He puts a new set of clothes on his lap and hits the bathroom fully dressed. I remind myself that he hasn't been naked in front of a woman since his injury and he's probably a little anxious about it.

The theater is only a few blocks away, so we decide to walk over. I have to say, even though I miss my Adam, I love twenty-four-year-old Adam's enthusiasm. About every half block, he stops me and pulls me down for a kiss. I guess that's the kind of thing you don't do when you're thirty-eight, but I still think it's really sweet. I end up traveling the final half a block on his lap.

The ticket counter is a bit high for him, but he backs up his chair as he tells the ticket seller he wants two adult seats for the two o'clock show. He has to stretch a bit to grab the tickets, but I let him do it because I can tell he'd be offended if I tried to do it.

"Popcorn?" he asks me as we pass by the counter.

I actually love popcorn. It's super greasy and salty and delicious. However, in New York in 2008, Mayor Bloomberg passed a law saying that calories for foods need to be posted. So when I'm waiting in line for popcorn and see that the small bag I'm about to purchase has six hundred calories, that definitely takes some of the fun out of it. I've pretty much stopped eating popcorn. "Sorry," I say to Adam. "Too many calories."

He laughs at me. "You definitely do *not* need to watch your weight."

That sounds a lot like my Adam in 2013. He claims to be unable to see the ten pounds (okay, twenty!) that I need to lose. But it's not like I'm imagining the fact that my old pants won't button anymore. And anyway, if I didn't watch my weight, I'm probably look like a sumo wrestler right now. Adam's response is that even if I did, he'd still think I was sexy. I really doubt it though.

The other thing about movies in 2013 is most theaters have stadium seating. My Adam calls stadium seating the bane of his existence. In the olden days, he could go to the movies and sit anywhere he liked, albeit in an aisle seat. With stadium seating, there are designated areas for wheelchairs and he feels like it's just way too close to the screen. Plus there are only a few seats next to those seats and if it's a crowded theater, they can get filled up.

Anyway, this place doesn't have stadium seating and is practically empty because of the holidays. There are literally three people sitting in the theater, and Adam says, "All the good seats are taken."

I smile at him, and think to myself, "I can't believe you've been making that same corny joke for fourteen years." But instead, I say, "Where should we sit?"

"This is actually an important question," Adam says. "Like, for us, as a couple."

"Is it?"

"It sure is," he says. "I mean, if you like sitting near the front and I like sitting near the back, then I don't see how this could possibly work out."

He's being cute, although I hate to tell him that either way, there's no way that we can work out as a couple. And he ought to know that. I haven't been secretive about the fact that I'm not here for the long term. It makes me a teeny bit nervous he's talking this way.

"So what do you think?" he asks me.

I point to a row in the mid-back of the

theater. "Let's sit there."

"You really are psychic," he says to me. "That is exactly the row I would have picked."

Of course, it helps a bit that I know exactly where he likes to sit in a theater from the several dozen movies we've seen together.

I get in to my own seat, and Adam transfers out of his wheelchair to sit next to me. When the previews start up, he puts his arm around my shoulders. By the time the movie starts, he's giving me these very meaningful looks, and I know what's coming. It turns out that it really didn't matter that I already saw *The Talented Mr. Ripley* twice, because I really don't get to see much of the movie at all. If you know what I mean.

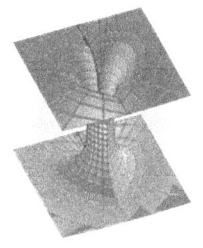

Seventeen

I don't get back to my parents' apartment until the evening. Adam wanted me to spend the night again, but I begged off, saying I needed to change my clothes. I've been intentionally vague about the details of how long I'll be staying here, but I know (well, *hope*) he senses that our time together is limited.

When I get back to the apartment, I'm sort of horrified. I shouldn't be though, because I now remember having thrown a party here on the night of New Year's Eve 1999. Still, I can't believe what a mess it is. There are beer bottles everywhere, chairs overturned, crumpled up napkins all over the floor. The entire apartment reeks of stale cigarettes and alcohol. Even though it's freezing out, I have to throw open all the windows just to air it out.

And what's maddening is that Claudia isn't even here. She just left the place this way. She doesn't even *care*.

The phone rings in the apartment and I nearly jump out of my skin. I reach for it, thinking it might be Adam, although it occurs to me as I'm picking up the phone that I never gave him my number. "Hello?"

"Hi, Claudia!" It's my mother. Holy shit, it's my mother! "It's your mother."

"Hi, Mom," I say, trying my best to sound … twenty-two.

"Thank you so much for bringing the paper in for us," Mom says. "I can't believe I forgot to cancel our service." Well, that explains the huge stack of newspapers nearly blocking the front door. Great job, Claudia.

"No problem," I say.

"Did you do something fun with Jed last night?" Mom asks.

I guess Claudia hasn't said anything about the break-up yet. And I'm not going to be the one to break the news. "Just some dinner," I say.

"That's nice," Mom says. "Now, Claudia, I know you're only twenty-two and you think everything is just about having fun, but you do have to start thinking about long-term commitments at this point. You don't want to wake up and find you're thirty-five years old and still single."

Try thirty-six years old.

I hate that I actually agree with my mother. I should have been thinking more about long-term commitments when I was in my twenties and the nice guys were still single. Then again, I wouldn't have met Adam if that happened. In any case, I can't show any sign right now that I think my mother is right.

"Mom," I whine, doing a remarkable impression of my younger self. "Will you quit it? I'm only twenty-two, not forty."

"All right, all right," Mom says. "Anyway, hold on. I'm going to put Daddy on the phone."

There's the usual shuffling on the other line, and I finally hear a loud, clear voice boom out: "Hello, Claudia!"

I grip the phone tighter. I forgot that in the year 2000, I would be talking to Don Williams, high-powered malpractice attorney, not Don Williams, stroke survivor. It's been so long since I've heard him speak without his words slurring into each other. My eyes start to tear up.

"Hi, Daddy," I whisper into the phone.

"What's wrong?" Dad barks into the phone. "Is that boyfriend of yours making trouble? I don't like him! I never liked him."

I hear my mother in the background, saying, "Don, please …" As for me, I'm at a loss for words. My father has no idea that in nine years, he's going to have a devastating stroke. That he isn't even going to be able to talk or eat for several weeks, and he'll be left with "mild cognitive deficits." That he'll need to rely on a four-pronged cane just to walk down the block.

Could I warn him? I want to, but what would I say? For years, Mom nagged him to get his high blood pressure taken care of. It's unlikely he'll take it seriously if his bratty twenty-two-year-old daughter tells him to do it. And really, the stress was probably a big contributor. What do I do? Tell him to cut back on his hours? He'll never do that and we'll just end up fighting. This trip to Florida is the only vacation he gets the whole year—I don't want to wreck it for him.

No matter what, he's going to have that stroke. There's nothing I can do about it. And that thought is just so depressing.

"I'm fine, Dad," I finally manage. "How are you doing?"

"Great!" he says. "It's eighty-three degrees down here!"

That's one thing that hasn't changed—the fact that my father loves telling me the weather in Florida while I'm stuck in freezing New York. These days, he texts me the Florida temperature on particularly snowy days in New York.

Dad hands the phone back to my mother, who comes back sounding a little breathless. "So,

Claudia, we'll be back mid-January. I know you're having issues with your roommate, so you can use the apartment if you'd like, but please don't bring other people over. And keep things clean. Okay?"

"Okay," I say, taking a second survey of the mess around me.

I'm furious with Claudia for how she left the place. For a moment, I imagine myself marching her to the broom closet and forcing her to tidy up, but the second I hang up with my mother, I start cleaning everything myself. Honestly, I just can't bear to see the apartment so messy. Another way I've changed in the last fourteen years—when I was Claudia's age, I wouldn't have cleaned up someone else's mess over my own dead body.

I just hope I don't come across any dried vomit.

I'm in the middle of vacuuming when Claudia breezes into the apartment, looking slightly hungover but probably not as much as she deserves to be considering how much she drank last night. She sees me cleaning and her face brightens. "You didn't have to do that, Beth," she says. "I would have done it."

She never, ever would have done it. She would have half-assed cleaning the apartment and it would have still stunk to high heaven of beer and cigarettes by the time our parents got back.

"Consider it thanks for your parents' hospitality," I say. Plus the two hundred dollars that I stole.

Claudia grins at me. "By the way, where were you last night, young lady? I thought you didn't know anyone in town."

I shrug. I'm not about to tell Claudia what happened between me and Adam.

"I never asked you," she says. "Do you have a boyfriend?"

"Yes," I say, not really wanting to get into this conversation.

"Really?" Claudia seems intrigued and I'm suddenly sorry I said anything. She's not the kind of person I want to confide in. "How long have you been together?"

"A year."

"Is it serious?"

I turn off the vacuum and straighten up. "Yeah, kind of. I mean, I'd like it to be. He's not as sure."

"How old is he?" Claudia asks.

"Thirty-eight."

"Seriously?" She makes a face. "That's so old! Doesn't he want to get married and have kids or something?"

"Apparently not," I say. I feel a lump rising up in my throat. I hate that Claudia is making me feel this way. But she's right. Adam isn't young anymore. Why doesn't he want me? What's he waiting for? What the hell is he fucking waiting for?

"Do you want to have kids?" she asks me. She squints at me. "Can you still have them? You haven't gone through menopause yet, right?"

I glare at Claudia. "Menopause?"

She shrugs. The crazy part is that she genuinely didn't mean to be insulting.

"I'd like to have kids," I say, the lump in my throat growing larger. As I say those words, I realize that my chances of becoming a mother are quickly slipping through my fingers.

"Well, just ditch him and find another guy then," she says as if it's nothing.

I want to ask her if she's ever been in love, but there's no point. I know she hasn't. She doesn't get it. I turn the vacuum back on, and thank God, she accepts that this is the end of our conversation.

***

When I'm satisfied that the apartment is spotless, I give Adam a call at the number I still have scrawled on the napkin. He picks up on the first ring. "Thank God!" he cries into the phone. "I forgot that I didn't have your number. I thought I was going to have to wait another two years to see you again."

I laugh. "I could give you my number, but it's my aunt and uncle's number. I'm staying with them for now."

"Give it to me," he says. "I'm not taking a chance of not being able to find you."

I give him the number, but it makes me a little nervous. I'll be gone in about six days, and I don't want him calling here to try to find Beth.

"Could I interest you in doing something touristy tomorrow?" he asks.

"Sure," I say.

"Museum of Modern Art."

"I hate art."

"Me too. I don't even know why I suggested that."

"Empire State Building," I say.

"I hate heights."

"Okay ..." I think a minute. "Museum of Natural History?"

"That has dinosaurs, right?"

"I believe so."

"Count me in then."

Adam wants to meet me at my apartment building, but I convince him to let me meet him at his place. The last thing I need is Claudia seeing him around here.

I realize that I have a new mission now in the year 2000. Young Claudia and Adam aren't going to happen, that's very clear. But I can still make a difference. If I can create a great relationship experience for Adam, then he'll have more self-confidence and The Bitch won't be able to destroy him. Maybe he'll have the courage to ditch her when things are going badly. Maybe I can even subtly warn him about her. All I know is that when I get back to 2013, things are going to be totally different. For the better.

Eighteen

My Adam never took me to the Natural History Museum, but he did take me to the Planetarium attached to the museum. He warned me in advance that he used to be "really into" astronomy when he was a kid.

He wasn't kidding about that. Adam mostly couldn't shut up through the beginning of the show. He kept leaning over and whispering things in my ear like, "The Big Dipper is actually part of the constellation Ursa Major," or "Sirius is the brightest star in the night sky." After doing this for about fifteen minutes, this guy sitting behind us hissed, "Will you shut up, please?" Adam sheepishly apologized and didn't say anything else through the whole show.

After the show was over and Adam was climbing back into his wheelchair, he said to me, "Sorry I'm such a dork."

"Don't apologize to me!" I said. "I love that you're a dork."

"Yeah, right."

"I do!" I insisted. "I would much rather have listened to you for the last half hour than Whoopi Goldberg." (Whoopi was narrating the planetarium show.)

"You're lying," he said, although he was smiling.

"I mean it," I said, tugging on his shirt so he'd come in close for a kiss. And I did mean it. Adam is crazy sexy when he's being a huge dork. "I insist that you teach me more about the constellations."

So we went through the planetarium exhibits and he talked my ear off about the stars and the planets and the big bang, but it was pretty cute. When you're in love with someone, they could be pretty much talking about anything and you'd be fascinated. That's sort of where we were at that point. It's where we still are.

***

The next morning, I find twenty-four-year-old Adam outside his building, waiting for me. I watch him scanning the streets, shifting in his wheelchair, and then his eyes light up when he sees me. He really seems to like me a lot. It's kind of flattering.

"You look great," he says to me, even though I'm bundled up in my mother's bulky black coat and look mildly Eskimo-esque. I decided against a hat, so my ears are slowly getting frostbitten, but at least my hair looks good. Well, it would if it weren't dyed mousy brown.

"Thank you," I say anyway.

"Okay," he says. "You ready to head out?"

I nod. "Let's go to the West Side and get the bus uptown so we end up on the right side of Central Park."

Adam smiles at me. "Thank you for not suggesting the subway. My friends are always convinced that I can make it work. Not gonna happen."

I learned that from my Adam. The subways in this city are not exactly accessible.

I quickly get the sense from Adam that he doesn't take the bus very often. The bus driver sees him and lowers the lift so that he can board, and Adam struggles a little to position himself. In 2013, he slides onto that lift effortlessly, but not in 2000. Two people get booted out of their seats so that he can position his wheelchair in the handicapped spots, and I can still hear Adam apologizing to them when I finally board the bus.

"I hate this," he confides to me as we travel uptown. I'm hanging on to the pole next to him because there are no seats left on the whole bus.

"You'll get used to it," I say.

"Says you, Psychic Girl." Adam shifts his weight in his chair and looks up at me. "You should sit."

"No seats," I point out.

Adam gestures down at his lap. "Perfectly good one right here."

I laugh and look around the bus. That's something my Adam never would have suggested. "Are you serious?"

"Definitely," he says. "Everyone on this bus is looking at me and feeling sorry for me because I'm a young guy who's disabled. I want them to be looking at me and feeling jealous because the hottest girl on the bus is sitting on my lap."

He raises his eyebrows at me as the bus comes to a halt. Before I have a chance to respond, he grabs me and pulls me into his lap. I can't help myself—I let out a squeal then cover my mouth because people really are looking at us now. But Adam doesn't seem nearly as bothered by it as he was a minute ago.

We were so distracted by each other that we probably would have missed our stop if Adam hadn't told it to the driver when we were getting on. The driver stops the bus by the museum and stomps his way to the back. When he sees me sitting on Adam's lap, he gives us this look, like, "Now I've seen everything." I quickly scramble to my feet and apologize. "There were no other seats," I say as Adam laughs.

It's a five-minute walk from the bus stop to the museum. I recognize the pillars of the old museum from a block away, although I'd mostly forgotten about the dozen or so steps to get to the front entrance. "I'm sure there's a handicapped entrance," I say to Adam.

"It's the law," he agrees.

We get about halfway around the block when we see a second entrance and this one has no stairs to get up to it, but instead there are stairs to get *down* to the entrance. It's a basement entrance with about eight steps. "You've got to be kidding me," I say.

"No, it's okay," Adam says quickly. "I can do stairs going down. They showed me in rehab."

He looks at the stairs a bit nervously and I'm guessing that despite being taught in rehab, this isn't something he's done a whole lot. But he's game to try, so I'm not going to stop him. My Adam once said to me, "It's not like I've never wiped out before."

He puts his hands on the push-rims of his chair and does a wheelie. He grabs the railing with one hand and uses it to guide him as he bumps his way down the flight of steps. When he lands on the ground at the bottom, he looks distinctly relieved. "Okay, that worked."

"Nice job," I tease him, hurrying down the steps after him.

"Thanks," Adam says, his face breaking into a smile. "All right, let's see these damn dinosaurs."

As a person who grew up in Manhattan, I've been to the Natural History Museum many, many times. It's pretty much a requisite place to go every single year on class trips. Eventually, you get so sick of the damn place, you feel like you'll just vomit if you see one more stuffed dodo bird.

Then at some point in your twenties, it doesn't seem quite as bad anymore. Like maybe you can appreciate it on a whole other level, when you can go to any exhibit you want and skip over all the boring ones. If you want to spend an hour just staring at the giant whale, that's allowed.

Adam is mostly excited about the dinosaurs, though. He stares up at the T. Rex in complete awe, his head tilted all the way back. "This is so cool," he breathes.

"It's sort of cool," I admit.

"Beth, it's a dinosaur!"

"It sure is."

"I thought it would be a little bigger

though, somehow," he says, cocking his head to the side.

"It's not big enough for you?"

"Well," he says thoughtfully, "you think of the T. Rex as being this giant monster dinosaur, crushing everything in sight under its ginormous feet. I mean, this is pretty big, but it's not, like, *that* big. It looks like you could probably fight with it a little bit."

I look from the huge dinosaur skeleton to Adam. "Really? You think you could fight that thing?"

"Well, maybe not *me*," he admits. "I'd probably be pretty screwed if I went back to prehistoric times. This chair isn't equipped for Cretaceous terrain." He looks back up at the T. Rex. "No, I'd probably have to outsmart it."

I start laughing outright. "How would you outsmart it?"

"What?" Adam snorts. "You don't think my intellectual capacity is a match for a dinosaur?"

"Well, the brontosaurus *did* have two brains."

Adam beams at me. "Impressive. How did you know that?"

"I've been to this museum a lot," I say, rolling my eyes. "I went pretty much on every class trip during elementary school."

"You're so lucky."

"What? Didn't they have any dinosaur bones in Akron?"

Adam breaks his gaze away from the T. Rex and gives me a funny look. "I never told you I grew up in Akron."

Crap. "Yes, you did."

"I'm pretty sure I didn't."

We just stare at each other for a minute. I can't even begin to imagine what he thinks of me. Somehow I know all this information about him that he never told me. If situations were reversed, I'd be majorly creeped out by now. But Adam seems to be mostly accepting it with good humor. At some point, though, I'd imagine he's going to demand the truth.

"Let's go see the 'raptors," Adam says.

Not now though, apparently.

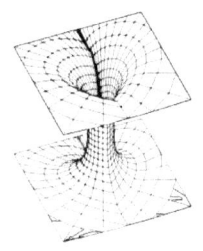

Nineteen

We spend the entire day at the museum, which is something I haven't done in ages. Adam asks me where I'd like him to take me to dinner, and I manage to mention Shake Shack and about five other restaurants that don't exist yet while Adam stares at me. Finally, I just mumble, "Wherever you want."

We eventually settle on a large chain restaurant that happens to be only a block away from the museum. It's pretty crowded when we get inside, and the hostess gives Adam a kind smile and tells us that she can offer us a table for two right away, with the caveat that it is way in the back of the dining area.

I look at Adam, who nods and says,

"Okay, let's do it."

This turns out to be a dire mistake. I wouldn't have predicted it, since my Adam generally has no problem getting across crowded areas. He is great at grabbing onto furniture to help propel him through tight spaces, and moreover, he has a pretty accurate sense of where his wheelchair will fit and where it won't. However, twenty-four-year-old Adam does not have that sense yet. He really has to struggle to get across the room, to the point where I'm getting embarrassed for him. The highlights include him knocking over an empty chair, and also him catching the legs of a woman's chair and causing her to spill water all over herself.

"I am so sorry," Adam says to her, red-faced.

I thought the classy thing for her to do would have been to not make him feel bad about it, but it looks like the woman was on a date herself and wasn't too thrilled about getting her skirt soaked in such a way to make her look like she had peed on herself. She just glares at him and snaps, "It's fine."

When we finally got to our table, Adam's shoulders slump and he comments, "Sheesh. It was really crowded there."

"You'll get better at it," I assure him.

He rolls his eyes. "Thanks. And this, by the way, is why I haven't been super eager to get set up on dates."

"That's a pretty shitty excuse, if you ask me."

"I didn't ask you." Adam flips his menu open with a snap to the page with the burgers on it.

By the time our drinks arrive (beer for him, a margarita for me), he's considerably less tense. As he takes a long sip of his drink, he says to me, "Sorry. I was being a jerk."

"Yeah, a little," I say, although I'm smiling.

"I just …" He tugs nervously at his earlobe. "Sometimes it sucks that now I'm the guy in the wheelchair."

I blink at him. "What do you mean?"

He smiles wryly. "You know what I mean. Like, at work, if someone wants to point me out to another person, they'll say, 'You know, Adam, the guy in the wheelchair.' That's, like, the easiest way to describe me now. And it's the only thing a lot of people see."

My heart aches for him. I wonder if that's what he thinks fourteen years from now too. He's never said anything like that to me. "That's not true."

"It *is* true," Adam insists. "I'm the same guy I always was, but now people get all awkward when they first meet me. Pretty much everyone does."

"Everyone?"

"Well, you didn't," he says thoughtfully. "Not even for a second, actually. That was why I thought ... maybe I had a shot with you."

I can't help but think about when I first met Adam in 2012, how I surely showed that awkwardness he described. But after a year, it's completely gone. "So that's what you like about me?" I tease him.

"It's not the only thing." He takes my hand across the table. "The truth is, I've always fantasized about a girl just like you. A sexy, older teacher."

I raise my eyebrows. "Older?"

"Well, older than me," he says quickly. "You're not old. At all."

"Nice save."

Adam smiles. "Seriously, though. I've fantasized about that since I was, like, thirteen."

"Have you ever fooled around with a professor in college?" I ask.

"What do you think, Psychic Girl?"

I look Adam over, from his disheveled hair to his shirt with the buttons mismatched. I don't need to be psychic to answer this one. "I doubt it."

He gasps. "I'm offended."

I shrug. "I'm just going with the odds. I mean, you were a computer science major, right? I'm guessing your computer professors were not very sexy."

"Mostly," he admits. "But there was one professor I had a total crush on: my operating systems professor junior year, Dr. Campbell. She was a total MILF."

"So how come you didn't hit that?"

Adam laughs. "You're adorable, you know that?"

"That's not an answer."

"Do you really need an answer?" He shakes his head. "I'm not the kind of guy who hooks up with professors. I was just lucky girls in my own class were occasionally willing to go out with me."

His self-esteem definitely isn't great. Even before the disability, it doesn't seem like he had a whole lot of confidence in himself, despite the fact that he's a fairly attractive guy. That's something that I might be able to fix. Starting right now. "You're actually very sexy," I say.

Adam snorts and doesn't respond.

"You are," I insist. "You just need … a few adjustments."

I move my chair around to the side of the table so that I'm right next to him. He inhales sharply as I place my hands on the fabric of his flannel shirt, with the buttons off by one. I start undoing and redoing the buttons for him as he watches, his eyes wide. I leave the top button undone so as not to choke him, and I straighten out the collar. As I do so, I see his Adam's apple bob as he swallows. "There," I say, brushing off my hands. "Perfect."

"Yeah," he breathes.

We stare at each other for another second, then he leans forward and starts kissing me. I have to say, Adam in either year is probably the most passionate guy I've ever dated, at least when it comes to me. We kiss for several more minutes until we hear the waiter clear his throat to signify that our food is ready. I'm not sure either of us is very hungry, though.

***

When I spend time with Adam, I can't help but compare him to the older version of himself:

1. My Adam is more comfortable with his disability. Twenty-four-year-old Adam is not comfortable yet. He doesn't think of himself as disabled, not really. I could see him blush when he asked the guard at the museum where the handicapped exit was located. My Adam wouldn't have been bothered—for him, it's a fact of life.

2. Twenty-four-year-old Adam is younger. Duh. Still, it's sort of amazing how that little fact accounts for such a

difference. At twenty-four, his skin is perfectly smooth and he's so full of energy. He's better looking at twenty-four. But at thirty-eight, he's sexier. The lines on his face and the gray hairs mixed in with the brown only make me want him more.

3. My Adam is more jaded. I hate to say it, but it's true. At twenty-four, he isn't waiting for the other shoe to drop. He isn't telling me I'd be better off without him. He just wants me.

4. Twenty-four-year-old Adam kind of doesn't know what the hell he's doing half the time when it comes to women. He tries, bless his heart, but he isn't any kind of Casanova and it's clear he never was. He means well, but he says the wrong thing *a lot*. I'm guessing that when we get further than just kissing, there's going to be a lot of fumbling. Not that my Adam is a Casanova, but I guess the extra maturity and experience keeps him from acting like a jackass.

I miss my Adam is the truth of it. The twenty-four-year-old version of himself is a nice guy, but he's not my boyfriend. I miss the guy I fell in love with a year ago. Half the time, I pick up the phone, ready to call him, and then I remember that he doesn't exist yet. And it almost makes me want to cry.

***

I'm on Adam's lap by the end of the meal. I'm running my hands through his hair and over his chest, and he's kissing me like he can't get enough of me. Ordinarily, I don't fool around with guys that I've been dating less than a week, but technically, I've already been with Adam many, many times. So I'm giving myself a free pass here.

"Your place?" I whisper in his ear as a somewhat flustered-looking waiter slides us the check.

He starts to nod, then grimaces. "Shit," he says.

"What?"

"I've got a super important meeting first thing tomorrow morning," he explains. "Big client. I've got to be able to, you know, perform well." He looks down at his legs. "Especially now."

I get what he's saying. Adam always said that he never wanted any extra slack at work because of his disability. But I can't hide how disappointed I am.

"I'll call you tomorrow," he promises, squeezing my hand in his.

As much as it pains both of us, we grab a

taxi and he insists on taking me back to my apartment. Except I don't want him to know where I live so I completely make up an address about five blocks from where my parents live. The second I see a building that looks reasonable, I quickly say, "That's it!"

I figured Adam would just have the taxi drop me off and ride it the rest of the way back since it's a pain in the neck to get his wheelchair out of the trunk, but instead, he insists on getting out to walk me to the door. Which would be really sweet if I actually lived here, which I don't.

"You really don't have to take me to the door," I tell him.

"Of course I do," he says. "It's dark out. What kind of gentleman would I be?"

"Yeah, but I don't want you to have to bother with your chair," I say, like I'm being nice about it. "Then you have to get back in again, right?"

"Nah, don't worry," he says. "I don't live that far away. I can make it without a cab."

"Are you getting out or not?" the cabbie asks us, obviously a little impatient.

He is. He gets back into his wheelchair, which I retrieve for him from the trunk, and he follows me to the building entrance, where he pulls me into his lap for a really lovely kiss, one that could just go on forever, as far as I'm concerned. It does make me sort of glad that I'm not in front of my parents' building though, where Claudia would be sure to somehow run into us.

"Good night," I whisper to him as I shakily get to my feet. For a second, I'm not certain my legs will support me.

"Good night," he says, still holding my hand as if reluctant to let go.

I figured that would be it, but then he follows me into the building lobby. Where there is a doorman who doesn't know who the hell I am. I need Adam to leave before this gets awkward. "Good night," I say again.

"Let me just make sure you get in the elevator all right," he says.

"I'm not five years old," I point out. I'm trying not to sound angry, but I'm definitely feeling a little agitated now. Especially since the doorman is giving us a funny look.

"Humor me," Adam says, smiling at me.

All right, now what the hell am I supposed to do?

The doorman has no idea who I am, but really, do doormen actually recognize all the residents of a building? I'm an attractive, well-dressed, Caucasian woman. I don't look even remotely suspicious. I bet if I just act confident, I can stroll right past him. Then I'll kill a little time in the elevators until I'm sure Adam is gone.

I push my shoulders back and move

confidently toward the elevators. I don't get very far before the doorman steps in front of me. "May I help you?" he asks.

I glance back at Adam, who is still freaking sitting there. *Why won't he leave?* "I'm just going up to my apartment," I say casually.

The doorman raises his eyebrows at me. "I'm sorry. And that is …?"

"Apartment 5E," I mumble.

"Are you a guest of the Fosters?" he asks.

"Uh huh," I manage.

"Let me buzz them for you then." The doorman goes over to the intercom. I turn around and see Adam still sitting there. If this is a game of chicken, I am totally losing right now. "And what's your name, miss?"

I swallow hard. "Uh, you know what? Never mind. I, uh … have some things I need to do first."

I run out of the building, my heart racing. Wow, that was embarrassing. I had no idea that doormen actually served such an important purpose.

Adam follows me out of the building, and when I turn to look at him, he's frowning at me. "You're not actually staying in that building, are you?"

Guiltily, I shake my head.

"I *knew* it!" he cries. "You had no clue where that cab was taking us, did you? You were just looking for some building that looked reasonable."

Wow, he totally had my number the whole time.

"Why don't you want me to know where you're staying?" he asks. He's trying to look me in the eyes, but I'm avoiding him.

"It's complicated," I finally say.

He sighs. "You have to admit, I haven't questioned you about most of your bullshit stories," he says. "I know you're hiding something from me, Beth. I'm not going to force you to tell me what it is, but I think I at least deserve to know where you live if you're going to be my girlfriend."

Something about his words tugs on my heartstrings. "I'm your girlfriend?"

His face colors slightly. "Well, not ... I mean, I thought ..." He takes a breath. "Do you *want* to be my girlfriend?"

I smile at him. "I think I might."

"Well, too bad," he says, returning my smile. "Because I'm already dating like five other girls."

I can see his shoulders relaxing and I know he isn't going to press me on the issue of where I'm staying. He's kind of a pushover.

"Fine," he says. "Don't tell me where you live. But I'm going to find out everything sooner or later."

"Yeah," I agree, just to appease him. In reality, I know there's no chance of that happening.

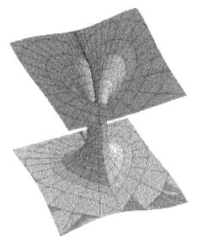

Twenty

I get nervous when I don't hear from Adam the next morning. Not that I'd ever expect to hear from a guy I just met every single day, but he told me that he'd call me and the Adam I know always keeps his promises. Plus we both know my time here is limited. Except he doesn't know quite how limited. I've literally got less than five days left to make him feel good enough about himself to resist The Bitch and her evil red curls.

I consider calling him a few times, but I'm sure he won't like that. Men don't like women who are clingy, who make the first call two times in a row. It doesn't matter that Adam and I have actually been dating for over a year—this Adam doesn't know anything about that. And he's twenty-four years old, which means he's probably even less thrilled than my Adam about making a commitment.

So instead I walk around the city, trying to distract myself from thinking about the present and especially the future. I visit a couple of my favorite stores that have closed down in the last decade. I get lunch at this great Chinese restaurant that burned down in a fire in 2005. Everyone should get one chance to hang out in the past for a couple of weeks.

When I get back to the apartment around dinnertime, Claudia is already there, sitting on the living room sofa. She's wearing tight boot-cut jeans and a tank top, and I can't help but admire how damn flat her stomach is. Damn gravity — why can't I look like that anymore? And trust me, she is not on a perpetual diet.

Then I notice her face — she's crying.

"What's wrong?" I ask her, grabbing the box of tissues from the kitchen counter that we nearly emptied after Jed cheated on her.

"Got rejected for another commercial," she sniffles, wiping her eyes with the back of her hand. She's got mascara dripping down her cheeks. "It was a Revlon commercial. It's so unfair — I use all their products!"

"Well, maybe they think you're already doing a great job advertising their products," I say, settling down on the couch next to her.

Claudia gives me a look like she doesn't think I'm funny. "I don't know what I'm doing wrong," she whines. "How am I supposed to be an actress if I can't even get a part in a stupid commercial?"

"Well," I say thoughtfully. "Maybe you shouldn't be an actress?"

"It's such a great job, though," Claudia says. "I mean, you look like you used to be really pretty. Didn't you ever consider becoming an actress?"

Sometimes I honestly wonder if Claudia says stuff to me like that on purpose, just to piss me off. She doesn't seem like she's trying to be a bitch. I guess it just comes naturally to her. This is probably why I had so few female friends in my twenties.

"I think acting is a waste of time," I say. "You have to be lucky to make it big. And let's face it, you're not lucky."

Claudia leans back against the sofa and closes her eyes. "Yeah, that's for sure. But I don't want to be a waitress for the rest of my life."

I feel a sudden rush of sympathy for my mother. I can't believe I was so difficult. "Claudia, you went to college. I'm sure there are things you could do besides waiting tables."

"Like what?"

"Like teaching, for instance."

"No, thanks," Claudia says. "That's a job for old maids."

If I strangle her right now, would that be committing suicide? "It's actually a really rewarding, stable career."

Claudia raises her eyes. "Wait, are you a teacher?"

I'm almost hundred percent sure I've already told her that, but the difference is that this time she's actually listening. We spend the next hour talking about options to get her teaching degree, and by the end, she actually sounds pretty enthusiastic. Of course, she's so lazy and spoiled that part of me feels like she's never going to go back to school in a million years.

And then I remember that she already did it.

***

I'm minutes from sliding into my bed that night when the phone rings. Claudia left a couple of hours ago, so I feel safe answering it. "Hello?"

It's Adam. "Tomorrow night. You. Me. Pizza."

"Awfully short notice, Mr. Schaffer," I say, even though it's clear to both of us I have no intention of saying no.

"You gonna make me eat a whole pizza all

by myself?"

I laugh. "I guess I can't allow that to happen."

I can almost hear him smiling on the other line. "I'd offer to come to your place," he says, "but I don't want to disturb you in your Fortress of Solitude. So would you like to come here?"

"Sounds good," I say. We're both silent for a minute. I picture him lying in his bed, holding his cordless phone to his ear. Before I can stop myself, I blurt out, "What are you wearing?"

Adam laughs. "A silky black nightie."

"Come on, you're no fun."

"Fine," he says. He sounds like he's checking. "I'm wearing plaid boxer shorts and a T-shirt left over from college."

"NYU," I say, then I curse silently. Why do I keep doing that?

"Right again, Psychic Girl," he says, although he doesn't sound angry when he says it. I imagine him lying in bed, wearing his old gray T-shirt with the purple NYU logo with the torch in the middle. He loves that shirt even though it's covered in holes … except it probably isn't covered in holes yet. The purple lettering probably hasn't even faded. "And pray tell, what might you be wearing?

"Oversized black T-shirt," I say.

"Sexy," Adam says. "And how about under that?"

"Nothing," I breathe into the phone.

I can almost hear him swallow on the other line. Two years. It's been two years since he's been with a woman.

"Maybe I'll bring a change of clothes tomorrow," I say.

"You read my mind again," he says.

We hang up, and I lie down in bed and try to sleep. Whenever I close my eyes, I see Adam. And I'm not even sure which version of him I'm imagining anymore.

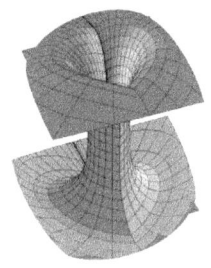

Twenty-One

When I get to Adam's apartment the next night, he immediately pulls me into his lap and starts kissing me. It startles me because my Adam is affectionate, but not nearly to this extent. I like it, although I get the feeling it would probably eventually drive me nuts. When you're dating someone for a year, you don't want them constantly pulling you into their lap.

The smell of hot pizza comes in from the living room. Like most New Yorkers, I'm kind of a pizza snob (and a bagel snob). I love a thin, crisp crust coated with mozzarella cheese and lots of oil. I'm sorry, but the Chicago deep-dish pizza just doesn't do it for me. And a calzone is not a calzone without ricotta cheese—people in other cities just don't seem to get that.

As Adam transports us to the living room, I see he ordered from Mike's, which is one of my favorite pizza chains. There's a Coke and a Diet Coke sitting on his coffee table next to the pizza.

"I suppose the regular Coke is for you," I say.

"Ladies' choice," he says.

And I take the Diet Coke. Because young Claudia's figure may be able to handle the extra three-hundred calories in that bottle of Coke, but mine definitely can't.

"Do you have any music to put on?" I ask him. Maybe it has to do with eating in restaurants too much, but I love having music on while I eat.

"Oh …" He gestures at a small CD tower in the corner of the room. Wow, CDs. How quaint. "It's mostly classical … do you like Mozart?"

Only when I have my migraines. The rest of the time, it reminds me of having a migraine—kind of a developed association. "Not a whole lot," I admit.

"Sorry," he says. "What kind of music do you like?"

"I love Peter Frampton," I say.

Adam just stares at me blankly and shakes his head. "Who?"

I can't believe my ears. "You know—Peter Frampton! 'Baby, I Love Your Way'? That's my favorite."

He just shakes his head again. Oh, well, it's not like Adam and I ever shared a great love for music. Although in 2013, he at least seems to know who Peter Frampton is. Maybe his music tastes matured.

It's a little hard to focus on the pizza, knowing what's going to happen after. Well, I don't really *know*. Adam may joke that I'm psychic, but I'm definitely not. Will we just do a little more kissing? Will he try to take things further than that? I sort of hope it's the latter. While I like kissing as much as the next girl, I'm really missing Adam's famous oral sex. I could definitely use a little stress relief right now.

"Sorry I didn't cook for you or anything," Adam says. "I know takeout pizza is kind of lame."

"Men cook?" I joke, even though I know, of course, that Adam is actually a great cook.

"I cook," Adam says defensively. "Or at least, I will, once I get a kitchen that's decent. This one's terrible, but I haven't been able to find any apartments to rent that are … you know …"

"Wheelchair accessible?"

"Right," Adam says, blushing slightly. "I've got this agent looking for me and her last suggestion was that I move into this senior housing development. I should probably fire her."

"Why don't you buy a brownstone?" I suggest. I'm giving all sorts of helpful advice lately, aren't I? "You can afford it, right?"

"Yeah," he says, giving me a funny look. "I can, but ... I don't know. I'm too young to buy a house."

"Look at it as an investment."

"An investment," he repeats.

I shrug. "It's nice to have a place to call home, isn't it? Do whatever you want with it?"

Adam glances in the direction of his kitchen. I happened to notice that his bathroom isn't terribly accessible, either. He's got a grab-bar next to the toilet that I guess they let him install, but the sink and vanity mirror are far too high. He must have to stretch to even wash his hands.

"You're right," he finally says. "I'll look into it."

I get two slices of pizza in me before the make-out session resumes. He pulls me back into his lap, but I can sense he's a little bit nervous. I can feel his hands shaking slightly as he runs them over my back. "Listen," he whispers. "I better tell you something."

I stare into his brown eyes. I watch him as he takes a deep breath. "I told you that you're the first girl that I've ... you know, *anything*, since my accident."

"Yes …"

"So the thing is …" He lowers his eyes, unable to look at me anymore. "I can't … you know. I mean, I *can*. I can get hard. It's just not … enough. Not for long enough, not hard enough." He lets out a sigh. "My doctor told me when there was a girl in the picture, I should call and they'd get me some pills. So this morning I called, but they can't get me in till next week." He tries to smile. "So next week, I'll be totally good. But right now, I'm kind of … out of commission."

"Oh," I say. I don't bother to tell him that I'll be gone by the time he gets in to see the doctor.

"I'm really sorry, Beth," he says. "If I knew I was going to meet you, obviously I would have … been prepared."

"No big deal," I say, trying to smile.

He hangs his head. I guess it's not easy to admit to your girlfriend that you can't maintain an erection. I can tell he feels really bad about himself right now, and I guess I don't blame him. God only knows what The Bitch would have done in this situation.

"Hey," I say, "we've only known each other a week. Who says I was going to let you score anyway? What kind of slut do you think I am?"

Adam rewards me with a very tiny smile.

"It's okay, really," I insist.

"Well, I thought," he begins. "I mean, we can't have regular sex, but I thought that we could ... I mean, that *I* could ... you know, pleasure you ..."

He's looking at me intently now. He's offering me oral sex. "Have you ever done that before?" I ask, although I'm afraid to hear the answer.

"Yeah," he says defensively. Then adds, "A couple of times."

This has the potential to be not so good. But, hey, maybe it'll be great. Maybe Adam has a natural talent for eating girls out. I mean, he's certainly really talented at it in 2013. "All right," I say. "Let's do it."

Adam's face lights up and the embarrassment of a few moments ago is forgotten. He wheels in the direction of his bedroom, and stops when his footplate hits the bed. My Adam usually lifts me gently off his lap onto the bed, but this Adam isn't quite as good at it—he pretty much just shoves me off his lap and I stumble a little, although I catch myself before I end up on the floor.

I help him out by pulling off my jeans and my underwear. I look at Adam, who is wringing his hands together nervously and tugging on his earlobe. I lie down on the bed, spread my legs, and close my eyes. Something about this feels like I'm going in for a speculum exam or something.

Adam dives in fast—too fast. He doesn't tease me or toy with me like my Adam always does. He gets his whole face in there, so he gets an A+ for enthusiasm, but he's not even remotely in the right area. Well, he's *remotely* in the right area, but it seems like he's missing the mark more than he's hitting it. Worse, after tolerating this for a few minutes, I notice that he's singing.

"Are you *singing*?" I ask, lifting my head.

Adam lifts his head. "Sort of," he admits, blushing. "I read that you're supposed to write the alphabet with your tongue, so I've been doing that. But I lost my place so I was singing it to get back on track."

Are you kidding me? How is it possible that a man who's given me the best oral sex of my life could be this bad at eating me out? He's *awful*.

"Listen," I say. "Don't be offended, but can I give you a few tips?"

Adam nods eagerly.

"First," I say. "Don't sing. You can hum, like blow air, but no singing. Really."

"Sorry …"

"Don't apologize, just listen," I say. "Also, don't dive in like that. You have to start slow, kiss my legs and my thighs and my stomach, blow hot air on me, don't just go straight for the clit. And when you get to the clit, go at it from the side, at least at first."

"Can I write this down?" Adam asks.

I glare at him. "No."

"Sorry," he says sheepishly.

"Just listen to me, okay?" I say. "If you're going to the alphabet, you don't have to make every letter like six inches high. Make some of them big, some of them small. You don't have to always move your tongue that much if you're hitting the right spot. Also, you're allowed to suck on me, but ..." I need to put in a disclaimer here: "Not too hard."

"Right," he says, and I can tell he wishes he had a pen and paper.

"Also, you can use your fingers," I tell him. "If you can't penetrate me ... the usual way, then you can do it with your finger while you're licking me. And if you're not using your fingers for that, you should be touching me. You could put your hands under my ass to bring me closer to your face."

Adam nods soberly.

"Most importantly," I say, "when I get close, you keep doing whatever you're doing. Do not stop. I repeat, do *not* stop."

Adam nods again. "I'm going to make this great for you."

That remains to be seen.

He makes a second attempt, this time following all my suggestions. It's substantially better, but still nowhere near as good as he is in the year 2013. I guess he gets in a lot of practice between now and then, but I don't want to think about that.

After I climax, he transfers into bed next to me, smiling nervously. "Was that okay?"

"Much better," I say.

He pulls me into his arms and his chest hairs tickle my shoulder. "That was so great," he says.

I laugh. "Was it?"

He nods vigorously. "I was so scared I wasn't going to be able to satisfy you. It's amazing that I could give you so much pleasure just with my mouth."

Well, it wasn't that *much* pleasure. Then again, my standards are pretty high these days, which is his own fault. "You were great," I say.

"I'm going to practice," he says. "As much as you'll let me. I love seeing you cum, Beth. There's nothing sexier."

I can tell he means it. If I were staying here, I bet he'd work his ass off trying to get good at this particular skill, just to give me pleasure. It's something he has in common with his older self.

***

Adam takes the next day off from work so he can spend it with me. He suggests a restaurant called Blue Hill in the village for lunch and I get really excited. "Oh my God," I squeal. "I heard Obama ate there."

"Who?" Adam asks.

Oh, right. He doesn't know who Barack Obama is. "I mean, Bono," I say. Bono existed in 2000, didn't he? Yeah, I'm pretty sure *The Joshua Tree* came out in the eighties.

"The place just opened," Adam says.

"Maybe I'm thinking of somewhere else," I mumble.

"Somehow I doubt it," he says.

At the restaurant, we brainstorm about things we want to do that day. He acts like I'm a tourist, but of course, I'm not. I've lived in this city my whole life. Plus it's too cold for a lot of the best activities. It's not snowing, but there were a couple of snowflakes falling as we walked to Blue Hill, which landed on Adam's shoulders and quickly dissolved.

This restaurant doesn't cost nearly as much as it surely does in 2013, so I pull out my wallet when we finish and offer to pay the bill. "Not a chance," Adam says.

"Come on," I say. "You paid for dinner last night."

"You mean the *pizza*?"

I shrug. "Why won't you ever let me treat you?" I wave my wallet at him. "I have the money, it's okay."

Adam looks at me like he's about to respond, but then he frowns. "Beth?"

"Yes?"

"Why do you have Claudia's driver's license?"

Crap. Why didn't I just let the guy pay? I try to put my wallet away, but he yanks it right out of my hand. I watch him as he scrutinizes my driver's license. The only positive thing I can say about this is that my hair is darker now than in the photo, so the picture probably looks more like young Claudia than it does like me. Except, like he said, what would her driver's license be doing in my wallet?

"Is this a fake?" he asks me.

"What?" I ask, my mouth dry.

"It says it expires in 2016," he points out. He shows me the license. Issued in 2012, expires in 2016.

"Right," I say, and I take the opportunity to pull my wallet out of his hand before he can start looking at the credit cards. What would he say if he saw card after card issued to Claudia Williams, all expiring about fifteen years from now? "It's a fake ID. That's why I confiscated it."

"But she's twenty-two," he says, sounding mystified. "Why would she need a fake ID?"

"Actually, she's only twenty," I lie.

Adam is still frowning. I can tell he doesn't entirely believe me, but he's not sure what to make of the whole thing. Finally he leans forward, like he's trying to read my face. I do my best to look impassive.

"Here's the thing," he says. "I'm dating this really great girl. She's funny, she's smart, and she's really, really sexy. But she won't tell me a damn thing about herself."

I clear my throat. "Sounds frustrating."

Adam shakes his head at me. "What would you do in my situation, huh, Psychic Girl?"

I can't even blame him for being upset with me. And what's worse is that I've got two more days left with him. It's not long enough. How am I going to build up his confidence when we've got only two days left and the guy doesn't even trust me?

That's when I see it: the bolt of lightning that splits his face in two. For ten years, that's meant only one thing.

Adam notices the look on my face and his expression changes to one of concern: "Beth? What's wrong?"

"Migraine," I manage. The pain hasn't started yet, but I know it's just a matter of time. And there's zero chance of getting any rescue medications other than an ibuprofen. I don't have health insurance in this year, and my 2000 counterpart hasn't yet been blessed with migraines.

"Is that like a headache?" Adam asks, his brow furrowed.

When I had my first migraine in the future, while dating Adam, he knew exactly what to do. But he doesn't seem to have that experience yet. I'm going to have to explain it all to him, which is the last thing I want to do while on the verge of a pounding headache. "It's like the worst headache you can imagine. Horrible pain, nausea … the works."

"Tell me what to do," he says.

He brings me back to his apartment in a taxi. Just as the taxi arrives at his building, the first jab of pain hits me. The world suddenly becomes painfully bright and I shut my eyes tightly. "Hey," Adam says, nudging me. "You okay?"

I shake my head.

He has to ask the driver to get his wheelchair out of the trunk while I sit in the cab with my eyes shut. After a minute, I hear him pull open the door. I crack my eyes open and see him sitting there, gesturing at his lap. "Hop on," he says. "You don't even have to open your eyes."

I comply, and he gives me a somewhat bumpy ride upstairs. Each bump is a little bit of agony. I am so grateful when we arrive in his bedroom and I can climb into his bed. The little jabs of pain have turned into a distinct pounding and the nausea is starting to rise. I feel like I might throw up.

"Tell me what to do," Adam says softly.

"Turn off all the lights," I instruct him.

He goes around his apartment, shutting off every light, even the ones that are too far away for me to notice. He closes the blinds in the bedroom, then reports back to me. "What now?"

"Mozart," I whisper. "Do you have any Mozart?"

"Yes, of course," Adam says. My eyes are closed but I hear him fumbling through his CD cases. At one point, a stack of them falls over and I cringe at the noise. But finally, I hear Mozart playing softly on his stereo. The gentle sound relaxes my shoulders.

"Anything else?" he asks.

"Lie with me," I murmur.

He complies. He transfers into bed beside me and tentatively puts his hand on my back. I move toward him and he wraps his body around mine. "Is this okay?" he asks me.

I nod.

I know I'm supposed to be working on making him love me today, but instead we spend the entire rest of the day in bed, his body entangled with mine, soothing away my horrible pounding headache. After a few hours of this, my headache is completely gone. Nobody is able to get rid of my migraines like Adam.

***

Adam brings me dinner in bed that night, which is very sweet of him, even though it's just a bag of bagels and cream cheese. I love the smell of freshly baked bagels. I remember a few months ago, Adam brought home a bag of particularly fresh, piping hot bagels, and I took one and cuddled it against my cheek. He still makes fun of me for that one, but seriously, that was one snuggly bagel.

"You didn't have to do this," I tell Adam now.

"Of course I did," he says. "You're the sickie."

And he insists on spreading the cream cheese on my bagels for me, even though it's way too much cream cheese and I'm sure it's not low fat. And I read once that eating a bagel is like eating eight slices of bread. Under ordinary circumstances, I try to stay low carb, and now after a week of looking at my twenty-two-year-old self's figure, I'm especially depressed about my weight situation. But somehow I still can't resist fresh bagels.

He hands me a bagel and I take a bite. "Amazing," I say. "You should be a chef."

Adam sticks out his tongue at me. I don't know whether it's how cute he looks at that moment or just the fact that I miss my boyfriend so much, but I put down my bagel, straddle him on his lap, and start kissing him. I guess he wasn't that hungry because he suddenly seems totally uninterested in bagels.

After a few minutes of kissing, Adam whispers in my ear: "Let me go down on you again."

"No," I say, shaking my head. "Your turn."

Adam clears his throat and looks away. "Uh, I told you that I can't, you know, feel it anymore. So it's nice of you to offer, but it's not going to do much for me."

"That's not what I meant," I say.

He frowns at me and that's when I lower my lips onto his earlobe. I hear him gasp, presumably unaware that it would have this impact on him. I'm guessing girls had sucked on his earlobes before, but maybe they got more sensitive after his injury.

A few seconds later, I've got him squirming and gasping for air as I run my tongue over his left ear. He slips his fingers under my shirt, pressing his palms firmly into the bare skin of my back. His eyes start to water and he squeezes them shut. I keep going, the way I've learned to after dozens of sessions with my boyfriend, and wait until the moment when he literally seems to lose control and squeezes all the breath out of my chest. Then he slumps down in his wheelchair, staring at me through hooded eyes.

"Whoa," he says breathlessly, clinging to me so that I can't escape from his lap.

There's a layer of sweat on his brow, which I wipe off gently with my fingers. "You enjoyed that, I take it."

He grins at me. "Do I have to dignify that with an answer?"

"It would be nice."

"I enjoyed it," he says. "That was fucking incredible, actually. *You're* incredible."

"Why, thank you, Mr. Schaffer."

He reaches out and brushes a strand of hair away from my face. "I'm really starting to fall for you, Psychic Girl," he murmurs.

Then he buries his face in my neck and I hold him close to me. He's definitely really into me, that's for sure. I wonder if maybe I overdid the earlobe thing. Oh, well.

***

Here's the thing:

Let's say my plan works and I do such a great job boosting Adam's confidence that The Bitch can't destroy him the way she did. Great news, right?

Except it has occurred to me that if Adam

doesn't develop commitment issues around this girl, that means he might not still be single at thirty-seven years old, when I first meet him at that dinner party. He might be married with kids by then.

I've thought about that possibility a lot. Losing Adam.

If that happens—meaning, I fix him and he meets someone else—I'll come back to 2013 and I'll be single. More single, because I won't even have Adam in my life. It really sucks, but at the same time, at least that way Adam will be happy.

I want him to be happy, even if he can't be happy with me. I mean, I'd rather he'd be happy with me, but at least he'll be happy.

I can live with that.

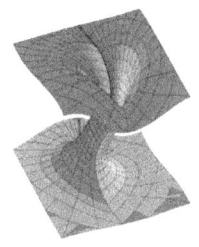

Twenty-Two

I end up spending the night at Adam's apartment, and when I wake up in his bed the next morning, I feel really disoriented. I'm waking up next to my boyfriend, whom I know very well, but it's a version of him that I hardly know at all, and in an unfamiliar bed. I stare at his unlined face and my fists clench with frustration. I'm going back to 2013 tomorrow. Tomorrow! And while he seems to like me a lot or even be "falling for" me, I can't say for sure that I've made any lasting impact on him whatsoever.

Adam senses me watching him and his eyes crack open. He smiles when he sees my face. "Hey there, you," he says.

"Hey, yourself," I reply.

He runs his fingers over my cheek, just gazing at me for a minute. "You are so sexy first thing in the morning."

He's such a liar. My hair is a rat's nest and my eyes are puffy. I'm pretty much the opposite of sexy.

But we're on the right track. I think about some possible romantic activities we can do today, something that will help seal the deal. "Any thoughts on how you'd like to spend the day?"

"Yeah, I gotta go to work, lady," he says. "Some of us aren't on perpetual vacation."

"But …" I start to tell him that tomorrow I'll be leaving, but I have a feeling that will result in a conversation I don't want to have. "Okay, then. I guess I'll fend for myself."

"Sorry," he says. "How much longer are you staying in the city anyway?"

I shrug. "It's sort of … flexible."

Adam smiles at me. "Well, I hope it's a long time."

As I watch him transfer into his wheelchair and hit his moderately inaccessible bathroom for a shower, I can't help but think that I'm going to miss this version of Adam. He's not quite the guy I fell in love with, but he's pretty great in a lot of ways. And he hasn't been ruined by some redheaded vixen.

After Adam leaves for work, I've got to figure out what to do with myself the rest of the day. It occurs to me that time traveling is actually kind of a nice way to take some vacation time. I've just gotten two weeks off and I'll come back to 2013 without having missed a day of work. Score.

The bad news is that I have no friends here and no working credit cards, so my options are a little limited. I make myself some toast and watch a little bit of boring daytime TV. I look through Adam's bookshelves, which contain some of the books he has now but is missing all the physics books he uses to help him in his inventions. I wonder when he decided to become an inventor. Somehow I thought it was something he'd always been interested in.

I eventually come across a large photo album. I pull it out and see tons of pictures of Adam and his friends, mostly from college. Photos from parties, a ski trip, a vacation in Cancun. I can't help but notice that there are no photos of Adam where he's in a wheelchair. Not even one. Eventually, that's going to change, though.

There's a photo of Adam standing between the World Trade Center Twin Towers, holding his arms out in the air. It occurs to me that there's still over a year and a half before those planes crash into the WTC. So many people died there. Could I somehow stop it from happening?

But no, I'm certain that I can't. The same way I couldn't stop Adam from getting hit by that car. Some events can't be changed.

But then again, here I am, making changes to the past. I have to believe that the things I'm doing here will have some impact on the future.

Or maybe I'm just kidding myself.

***

I end up taking a walk along Fifth Avenue, intending to mostly just window shop. Even though I have money left over that I swiped from my parents' stash, it seems like it would be awkward to take a bunch of new clothes back with me through time. I mean, what if taking that extra dress means that one of my toes won't make it back to 2013? Plus I'm not even sure how the clothes would go with me—last time, I just disappeared without warning.

Still, it's very hard to look at clothes all day without buying anything. I'm only human, after all.

The last stop on my excursion is Lord & Taylor's. I'm browsing the dress suits (my personal passion) when my eyes fall on an outfit that makes my jaw drop open. It's a gray Anne Klein two-piece suit with a skirt that falls to a respectable length, and a neck lined with little jewels. It's lovely, but that isn't why I can't stop staring at it.

This is the exact suit I wore during my interview to get into teaching college.

I remember how confident I felt in this suit, how for the first time, I believed that I looked like someone smart enough to be a teacher and responsible enough to be a good student. This suit is what helped me ace the interview. This suit helped me become the person I am today.

I don't even bother to try it on. I pay cash for the suit in young Claudia's size (size two—damn her!), intending to leave it in her closet. She'll never know I bought it for her. But when she needs it, it will be there.

I get back to my parents' apartment by five o'clock, clutching a shopping bag with my new suit carefully folded inside. As I walk in the door, I hear the phone ringing and I have a feeling I know who it is. I run for it and catch it on the sixth ring. "Hello?" I answer breathlessly.

"It's Adam," he says. "I'm glad I caught you. Are you busy now?"

"No …"

"Great," he says. "I need you to meet me somewhere."

Nice timing. I cringe at the thought of heading into rush hour traffic, but I remember this is my last night in 2000. I have to do whatever Adam asks of me. "Okay, where?"

Adam recites an address for me that's so familiar, it makes my heart start pounding. "Can you repeat that?" I ask, hoping I heard wrong.

He repeats the address. And it's exactly as I heard it the first time.

Adam just read me the address of his home in 2013.

***

I am officially freaked out.

I'm not kidding. Why in hell would Adam want me to meet him at the place where he lives in the future? How does he know that he lived there? Has he discovered my little scheme and wants to call me on it?

Freaked out is probably an understatement.

I'd love to grab a taxi, but at this hour, they're going to be hard to find, and I'll likely sit in traffic for hours. The subway, on the other hand, will be a quick ride.

I don't love the subway in New York. First, it smells like urine. I've never been on a subway car that didn't smell at least faintly of urine. Or beer mixed with urine. Second, I get groped on the subway with surprising frequency. It's happened to me at least five times in my life. I know that doesn't sound like a lot, but I think even once is too many times to be groped by a stranger on the subway.

But the good news is it's fast. And if you're freaking out about something your boyfriend just told you, there's no quicker way to get to him.

As soon as I get out of the subway station, I sprint the two extra blocks to find Adam at the brownstone. By this point, I'm really sick with anxiety. Especially when I see him in front of the brownstone and notice that he isn't alone but rather with a middle-aged woman with a hawk face and her black hair pulled back in a tight bun.

"Beth!" He waves to me enthusiastically. Well, at least he doesn't look angry.

"Hey," I say, and then I have to stop to catch my breath. I lean forward, clutching my knees as I gulp in air.

"You okay?" he asks. I nod wordlessly. "You didn't have to run. This is actually perfect timing. Naomi just got done showing me the place."

Naomi? I look up at the black-haired woman who offers me a cold, spidery hand. "I'm Naomi Levy, Adam's real estate agent."

I look at the brownstone then back at Adam. Suddenly, it all makes sense. He's thinking about buying the place! "I'm Beth Williams," I say.

"Will you be living here too?" Naomi asks

me, glancing from me to Adam with a judgmental look on her face.

"No," I say. Maybe I say it a little too quickly because Adam gets this hurt look on his face. If only he knew how much I'd be dying for him to ask me to move in with him in 2013.

"I just want to get her opinion," he says.

But he doesn't really need my opinion. I can tell he loves the house the second he shows me the side entrance that bypasses the steps to the front door. I walk through the empty rooms with him, imagining his furniture filling the bare spaces. He points to the spot where his ratty couch with the mustard stains sits in 2013. "I want to buy an extra-wide television and put it right there," he says.

"No," I say. "That's where the couch goes."

Naomi gives me a look when I say that. She probably thinks I'm being a controlling girlfriend or something, but I'm not. I'm just helping him out by telling him where his couch is supposed to be.

"So," Adam says, a grin spreading across his face. "Does that mean you like the place?"

I don't even hesitate. "Yes," I say. "This is your house. Put down an offer right now."

Naomi smiles at that, but she still has that odd look on her face. Adam says, by way of explanation: "Beth is psychic."

So now I sound like a complete nut job. Oh, well.

Adam fills out a few forms for Naomi before she locks up the house and tells him that she'll get back to him when she hears from the owners. Adam can't stop smiling. "I really like this place," he says. "I really do."

"You're going to be really happy here," I say, settling down on the steps of the brownstone so that I can look him in the eyes.

"Thanks for the vote of confidence, Psychic Girl," he says. He leans in and pecks me on the lips. He means to peck me on the lips, at least. It evolves into a much deeper kiss than I think he intended. "Beth …"

"Listen," I say, pulling away from him. "Speaking of me being psychic and all, there's something I need to tell you."

"I thought you weren't psychic," he teases me.

"Adam, I'm serious," I say, which wipes the smile off his face.

I thought about this on the ride over. I don't know if I've accomplished what I needed to these last two weeks, so I have to take out some extra insurance. I have to warn him about The Bitch. Maybe if he sees it coming, she won't hurt him so badly. It's my last chance to help him.

"Adam," I start, "after me, there will be other girls …"

He grabs my hand off my lap. "What? Come on ..."

"I mean it," I say, shaking off his hand. "You're going to meet this girl who you're going to think is great. The greatest girl you've ever met. Maybe a redhead—I'm not sure about that part. She's going to be your first real relationship after your ... injury. And she's going to break your heart." I heave a sigh. "I just had to warn you so you don't get hurt."

I don't know how I expected Adam to react. But what he does is lean in and kiss me again. His breath feels so warm against my face. "I don't think we have to worry about that."

Maybe he thinks the psychic thing is bullshit or something, I don't know. But it's obvious he's not taking my warning seriously. "And why not?"

"Because," he says, "*you're* my first real relationship after my injury."

At that moment, as he kisses me on the steps of the house where he'll someday live, I realize three things, three immutable facts:

1. Adam's right—I am his first real relationship after his injury.

2. He is very much in love with me.

3. I am about to disappear suddenly, leaving him abruptly, and cruelly breaking his heart.

And that's when I finally catch on to the horrible truth:

I am The Bitch.

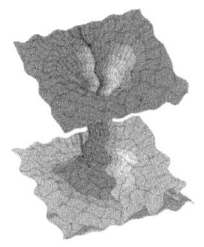

Twenty-Three

After my realization, I'm in shock for at least … I don't know, fifteen minutes. Adam keeps kissing me, but all the while I'm thinking that I can't believe I'm the one who ruined his life. Twice!

He must not know it's me in 2013. I go by a different name now, and my hair is different, and he's had time to forget my face. Plus I'm sure he doesn't expect me not to have aged at all in fourteen years. He just knows some girl named Beth made him fall in love with her in 2000, then disappeared abruptly and was never seen again.

All I know is I've got to make this right. I just don't know how.

"Hey," I say, disentangling myself from

him. "There's something else I need to tell you."

"If you could tell me who's going to win the Superbowl in February, that would be awesome," he says, still trying to lean in to kiss me.

"No, really," I say, putting my hand against his chest to keep him firmly at arm's length. (Although, technically, I *could* tell him who will win the Superbowl.) "This is important."

"Why are you so serious today?" he asks me, blinking his brown eyes behind his glasses.

"Because," I say, taking a deep breath. "I'm leaving soon. Tomorrow."

"Tomorrow?" His face contorts with surprise. "Why didn't you tell me? I would have taken the day off! I thought you said you were flexible?"

"I ... I have to get back to my class," I explain lamely.

"Okay." Adam nods, absorbing the situation. "That's all right. Look, I want to stay in touch. Do you think we can do the whole ... long distance thing? I'm a good pen pal."

"No," I say, shaking my head. "It's too far."

"How far?"

"Really far."

Adam isn't trying to kiss me anymore. He's just frowning at me and gripping the push-rims of his chair. "Where do you live? You can at least tell me that much."

Oh, Adam, I wish I could. I squeeze my eyes shut for a moment then open them again. "China."

"*China*?" He stares at me. "Seriously? You live in China?"

"Yes."

"Okay, fine," he says. "Say something in Chinese. Anything."

Crap. I search my brain. I must know one phrase in Chinese. It would be pretty pathetic if I didn't. "*Ni hao*," I finally come up with. And I can tell I haven't impressed him.

"You are so full of shit, Beth," Adam says, glaring at me, his hands folded across his chest.

I am. I am totally full of shit. This isn't working and I'm just insulting his intelligence and making him hate me. I've got to try a new tactic, one that seems to work like a charm on all men, including Jed and even my Adam.

"Listen," I say. "I know you think you like me and all, but … you just don't get it. You're only twenty-four and I'm a lot older than you. I'm older than you think I am and I want different things than you do."

Adam narrows his eyes. "How old are you?"

"I'm thirty-six," I admit.

Adam blinks a few times. I see that I've

actually taken him a bit by surprise—I think he thought I was thirty at the most. I can see him studying my face for lines, and I'm almost offended that he seems to believe me. "I didn't realize ..."

"Well, now you know," I say. "I want to get married and have kids right away, Adam. And you're only twenty-four and I know you don't want those things right now."

"Says who?" Adam retorts.

I sigh. "Come on. You're a *child*."

"A child? Is that honestly what you think of me?" Adam asks, sounding hurt. "I may be only twenty-four, but I want the same things you do. I want to get married and have kids too. And I know we haven't known each other that long, but I feel like I could see myself doing those things ... with you."

"Yeah, but not in the next year," I point out.

"I'm not afraid of commitment," he says. "I promise you."

Could I get that in writing, please? This is too unbelievable for words. The twenty-four-year-old Adam is perfectly willing to marry me and settle down, while his nearly forty-year-old counterpart doesn't feel ready. What the hell?

"You think you're ready ..." I begin.

"I'm ready," Adam says firmly.

I believe, at least, that he seems to think

that he's ready, that he believes he's willing to do anything for me. I'm not sure I can shake this guy.

"You don't care if I'm ready, do you?" Adam says. He shakes his head. "You want a commitment, but you don't want one from me."

I gesture helplessly at him. "You're too young …"

"Too young or too crippled?" I see the anger on Adam's face. He's starting to get bitter. I'm doing this to him. I'm creating that guy with all the lines on his face, all the gray hairs … the guy who can't settle down because he feels like he's not worth it. I see it happening and I'm just as helpless to stop it as I was that night when Jed hooked up with Crystal-Joy.

Maybe Adam was right when he said the future outcome can't be changed.

"You've got to believe me," I whisper, my voice hoarse. "It's not about you. It's about me. I have to go."

"It's not you, it's me," Adam muses. "How original."

"Adam—"

"Why don't you just be straight with me for once?" he says. His cheeks are pink but I don't think it has anything to do with the cold outside. "You don't want to be with me anymore. That's it, right?"

"No!" I say. "That's not it! I do want to be

with you. It's not what you think, I swear to you."

Adam focuses his brown eyes on me. "Then tell me the truth."

The truth. I can't tell him the truth. For starters, the truth is so crazy that he'll never believe it in a million years. And furthermore, didn't Adam say that if his past self found out about the time machine it could create some kind of, like, rip in the fabric of the universe or something? As much as I love Adam, I'd rather not destroy the whole universe. Unfortunately, that doesn't leave me with any other options. "I can't," I finally say.

"Why am I not surprised?" Adam says quietly.

He roughly grabs the wheels of his chair and takes off down the street. I watch the back of his head as it gets smaller and smaller as he moves further away from me. Then he turns a corner and he's gone.

***

I sit on the steps of Adam's brownstone far too long, hugging my knees to my chest. I sit there long enough that I'm worried I'm going to catch a cold, which I'll then bring back to the year 2013 and it will wipe out half the city because nobody has immunity. That seems pretty unlikely, though. Still, I don't want to get sick, so I get up and take the subway back to my parents' apartment.

When I get back, Claudia is all trussed up and ready for a night out on the town. It makes me tired just to look at her, wearing her tight skirt, low-cut shirt, and leather boots. Actually, it not only makes me tired, it makes me cold. I know she's just going to wear the thinnest of jackets when she goes out.

I can't believe the lengths I used to go to in order to look good. Or how often I used to go out at night. These days, my idea of heaven is a night at home with Adam, maybe watching a movie on the television with popcorn from the microwave.

Claudia perks up when she sees me. I was crying for a while on the steps of the brownstone, but my eyes have long dried up. And I wasn't wearing a ton of make-up that had the potential to get smeared, so I don't think it's that noticeable.

"Beth," she says. "Do you want to go to a club?"

Lord, no. "That's all right," I say. "I'm kind of tired."

"We're going to Limelight," Claudia says, whipping out a compact to check her lipstick. It's dark red. I used to have a bit of a goth thing going. "It's going to be really fun. I've totally seen some older guys there."

It occurs to me that "older" to Claudia probably means, like, twenty-nine. I'm not "older," I'm just old. Nobody closer to forty than to thirty goes clubbing. Or if they do, I don't think they'd be the kind of guy I'd want to meet. The word "pathetic" comes to mind.

The doorbell rings, and Claudia squeals, "It's him! It's him!"

"Who?" I ask, wracking my brain to try to remember who I was dating a week after New Year's in 2000.

"Anthony," Claudia says, a dreamy quality to her voice. "Oh, my God, he is *so* hot. Like, just so amazingly sexy. Incredible abs."

I still have no memory of the guy, which makes me a little disgusted with my younger self. This is why I'm still single. Because I spent my youth chasing jerks with great abs.

"Can you get the door?" Claudia asks me. "I just have to fix my hair." She pats her hair, which already looks perfect.

I go to answer the door and see a tall guy who practically looks like a bodybuilder—he is just that ripped. I can almost smell the testosterone oozing out of his sweat glands. "Hi," I say, turning my head slightly in disgust.

"Hi," he says, looking over my shoulder. "Is, um, your daughter home?"

I almost cry. This is just the worst day ever.

"She'll be out in a minute," I manage, not bothering to correct his mistake.

I leave Anthony in the living room to fend for himself and retire to the guest bedroom. I throw myself into the bed and bury my face in my hands.

I miss Adam. My Adam.

This twenty-four-year-old kid is nice enough, but I miss the man I fell in love with. I miss all the quiet nights Adam and I spent together in his house, just the two of us. I miss his sexy crow's feet and gray hairs. I want to see him now, so badly that it's physically painful.

And most of all, I want to spend my life with him.

Whatever I've messed up here, I've got to fix it. I've got to make it so that Adam trusts me and is willing to commit to me. And I am beginning to think there's only one way to do that. There's only one way to change the future:

I have to tell Adam the truth.

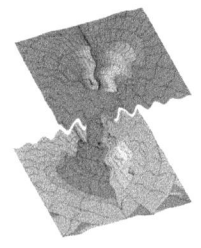

Twenty-Four

Warning: If you live in the universe and especially in the Milky Way galaxy, you may face the end of your existence soon. I mean, it might be totally fine and I might just be a Nervous Nelly, but it's probably best if you prepare yourself. Maybe buy some batteries and stock up on bottled water and canned foods.

I decide to wait until the next morning to call Adam. It's a risk because I have no idea at what time I'm going to get sucked back into that wormhole, but he was still angry with me the night before, so he needs time to cool off. It would be better if I could give him a few days, but I don't have that kind of time.

I wait until around ten in the morning

before I dial his number. Luckily, we're in the pre-cell phone era, so he can't screen my call. I hear a sleepy male voice on the other line: "Yeah, 'lo?"

"Hi, Adam," I say. "It's ... Beth."

"Oh." His voice is suddenly wary.

"Please don't hang up," I say. "I'm ready to tell you everything."

That perks up his interest. "Really?"

"Yeah," I say. "Can you meet me at that coffee shop by your house in an hour?"

"I'll be there," he says. He hesitates. "You're really going to tell me everything?"

"I am," I promise.

I just hope the universe doesn't get destroyed. But right now, I consider it worth the risk.

***

Adam is already at the coffee shop when I arrive. He's nursing a paper cup of coffee, and his eyes widen when I walk into the café. He doesn't look happy exactly, but not angry anymore either. It's hard to read his expression.

I don't bother to get my own cup of coffee, even though I could sure use it. I head straight for his table and slide into the seat across from him. "Hey," I say.

"Hey," he says. His eyes don't leave my

face.

"Thanks for coming," I say.

He nods and tugs on his earlobe. He's still clearly a little pissed off about yesterday. I guess I can't blame him, what with that whole lame China story. "So let's hear it."

The words are on the tip of my tongue but I'm having trouble pushing them out. "Maybe I'll get myself a coffee."

"Or you could just fucking tell me now," Adam says.

I deserve that. "Okay," I say. I pick up a napkin lying on the table and start shredding it into pieces. "Here's the thing, I'm not from here."

"You told me that."

"Right, but …" I take a breath. "I *am* from New York. I'm just not from … now."

Adam shakes his head. "What are you talking about?"

"I'm …" I close my eyes, summoning up all my courage. "I'm from the year 2013."

"*What?*"

I look around, expecting to see some big rip in the fabric of time, whatever that looks like. But no. We're all still okay. More or less.

"I know it sounds crazy." I don't think I even recognized quite how crazy until I saw the look on his face. "But you invented this time machine in 2013 and you sent me back in time to 1999." He's just staring at me so I hurry on.

"Well, first you sent me back to 1997 to keep you from getting into an accident on your bike, but then you ended up getting hit by a car anyway. And then I came back to 1999."

He's looking at me very intently, his expression unreadable. Does he believe me? I have no idea. "So why did you come back to 1999?" he asks.

"Because," I say, "I wanted to stop you from getting your heart broken by this awful bitch. Except I didn't realize the awful bitch was *me*. So I messed that one up as well. I just figured the only way to fix all this was to come clean."

There's a long silence between us. I continue shredding the napkin, just holding my breath, waiting to see what he'll say.

"Wow," Adam says finally, his eyes wide and unblinking.

"I know," I say.

He pushes his coffee across the table. "You must think I'm a complete idiot, don't you?" he growls at me. The anger in his voice now is about ten times worse than yesterday. "You promise me the truth and then you come up with this bullshit story about a fucking *time machine*? Are you kidding me with this, Beth? Or whatever your real name is."

"I'm not kidding," I insist. "It's the truth!"

"Here's a tip," Adam says through his teeth. "When you break up with a guy, it's better to tell him you don't like him anymore or you're interested in some other guy than tell him some bullshit story that insults his intelligence. I hurt my back, not my *brain*, despite what you seem to think."

"I don't think that," I whisper. This isn't going how I imagined at all. "I'm telling the truth."

"Fuck you," Adam says. He starts to push back from the table. He's going to leave. I can't let that happen.

"Please stop!" I cry. I fumble around in my purse. "Look in my wallet. None of my credit cards expire for twenty years! And you saw my driver's license the other day …"

"You mean your *cousin's* license that you took from her?"

"No, that was mine," I insist. "You have to believe me, Adam. I never mean to hurt you. The only reason I came back here was because I love you."

Adam looks up at me. He's got his hands on the push-rims of his chair, and I know he's going to leave. I don't think I can stop him anymore. "If you never meant to hurt me," he says, "then you fucked up big time."

With those words, he moves toward the exit. I stand up, watching him leave. That really didn't go well at all. Should I go after him? Try to convince him that I'm really telling the truth?

Except that's not going to happen. Because at that moment, I start to hear a whooshing noise in my ears. I'm leaving. I've run out of time and I haven't managed to fix a thing.

I race outside the coffee shop, looking for a place to hide. The whooshing is getting louder and I know I don't have much time. The world starts to spin and I can't see any obvious places where I can conceal myself. I check back in the café and see a sign for the bathroom. I make a run for it, hoping nobody will stop me for not having made a purchase.

It's a single ladies' bathroom. I shut the door behind me, knowing that I can't lock it or else nobody else will be able to get in. I stare at my reflection in the mirror, which starts to subtly distort. I shut my eyes as a sensation of vertigo overtakes me and I feel the ground disappearing below my feet.

The spinning becomes very intense for a few seconds, then it stops and I feel something solid underneath me. I am home.

I open my eyes, prepared to face Adam's dark, empty living room. Instead, I see my boyfriend sitting in his wheelchair a few feet away from me. My knees tremble and he grabs me to pull me onto his lap just before I collapse.

"Welcome back, Psychic Girl," he says.

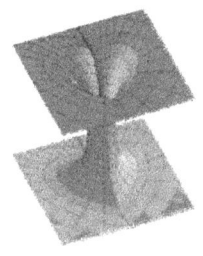

Twenty-Five

He knew. He knew all along.

The realization echoes in my head as I lean my head against Adam's shoulder, so much stronger and more muscular than it was when he was fourteen years younger. I shut my eyes briefly—this experience has completely wiped me out. I still feel that nausea, but since I hadn't eaten anything yet today, I don't feel like I have to throw up. Important time travel tip: don't eat on the morning of a trip.

Adam looks down at me, stroking my hair gently. My Adam. I missed him so much these last two weeks. I put my hand on his cheek, my fingertips touching the lines around his eyes. "Are you okay?" he whispers, a crease forming between his eyebrows.

I nod breathlessly.

He buries his face in my neck and I feel his stubble tickling me as he murmurs over and over again, "Thank God, Claudia, thank God ..."

He doesn't let go of me for several minutes, and when he finally does, his eyes are wet. "I was so worried," he says. "I thought about trying to stop you from going back, but I was scared that it would mean I'd somehow lose you. And that it might cause a paradox that would destroy the universe or something."

I shake my head. I think I've almost destroyed the universe like ten times in the last couple of weeks. "None of this makes any sense to me. I thought you didn't even believe me when I told you I was from the future."

"I didn't," he says. "Not at first."

"What changed your mind?"

He tells me the story in a quiet voice, the kind he uses when I'm having one of my migraine headaches. "I was angry at you that day in the café," he says. "I thought for sure you were messing with me, trying to come up with a guilt-free way to dump me. But then over the next few months, thinking about what happened with you, it started to make more and more sense. Then I ran into Claudia—well, *you*—in the grocery store and I realized how much she looked like you. That she essentially *was* you. Of course, back then you wouldn't give me the time of day."

"Sorry," I say sheepishly.

Despite everything, he laughs. "Yeah, you were a total bitch back then, weren't you?"

"I wasn't that bad," I mumble. But he gives me a look and I know he's right.

"So anyway," he says, "I realized at that point that there was only one way to get you back. I had to build a time machine."

I grin weakly. "No problem for a guy like you."

"Not exactly," he says. "I'd never built so much as a table before at that point. I had a lot to learn. So I bought a bunch of books and raw materials and … well, I started tinkering."

A realization hits me. "You became an inventor for me!"

"Well, yeah," he says, his ears growing slightly red. "But I ended up actually liking it. It was a great hobby. So, um, thanks for that."

I was always so touched when Adam made an invention just for me, like the musical rose or the foot bath. I had no idea that the biggest invention of his entire life was created solely for the purpose of bringing me to him.

"The thing is, I did the calculations a thousand different times," he says, his eyebrows scrunched together. "I was certain the machine was bound by the universal law of causality and couldn't change the events of the past. I was …

well, ninety-nine percent sure. I built the machine so that you could go back to the past and do the things I knew you'd already done then come back to an identical present." He looks troubled. "Except when you went back that first time, I realized that you *did* manage to change something."

"Right," I say. "You were supposed to get hit on your bike and I changed that."

"No, you didn't," he says, smiling a little sheepishly. "It always happened that way."

"But you said —"

"I said what I had to say to get you to go back to 1997."

I stare at him in surprise. He never meant for me to keep him from getting hit by that taxi. He knew that was inevitable and I wouldn't be able to stop it. But then what was the thing that had changed?

Suddenly, it hits me. I reach out and touch his chin. "Your jaw ... that scar ..."

He nods. "Right. When I discovered you really did change something, that's when I got nervous. That's why I was so moody last night. I'm sorry."

"I thought you were just mad about your jaw getting broken," I say.

"Well, I wasn't *thrilled* about that," he acknowledges. "But what really got me scared was that it occurred to me that certain untested hypotheses arising from the relative-state formulation of quantum mechanics *do* predict stochastic fluctuations in the time traveler's state vector upon return to the present. I realized it would be possible that some of the subatomic particles in the universe might be in slightly different configurations than they were right before you left."

I stare at him.

"Meaning under some circumstances, you *could* change the past," he clarifies.

"Oh." Sheesh. Time travel is complicated.

"So I got really worried about what would happen when you went back in time again," Adam says. "Especially for two whole weeks. I thought you might somehow change things for the worse in some unexpected way. I kept going back and forth in my head, wondering if I should try to stop you. I was going nuts over it. But I knew if you didn't go back, I wouldn't build the time machine and that would result in a major paradox. And then I might lose you."

"And the universe might get destroyed," I add.

"Yeah, that too," he says. He hugs me tighter to his warm body. "But mostly, I was just afraid of losing you."

He kisses me then, one of those long passionate kisses where our bodies seem to melt together. I'm sure he means what he's saying, although in all honesty, I think the universe coming to an end might be *slightly* worse than losing me.

In any case, it all makes sense, I guess, but there are still pieces that don't quite fit. I pull away from Adam, and look him in the eyes. "Why don't I remember any of this?" I ask him. "Like, from when I was twenty-two?"

He squints at me. "Don't you?"

Do I? I search the recesses of my memory and grab at vague recollections. Yes, there was an attractive older woman who was staying at my parents' house for a little while—I remember that part, although just barely. And there was that failed date with the retarded guy from my twenties. But no, it wasn't a retarded guy—it was just a guy in a wheelchair. Oh, God, that was *Adam*.

"None of it had the same meaning to you," Adam says. "It was just a few random events that happened fourteen years ago. But for me, it was meeting the love of my life."

When he says it, he takes my hand. The callouses are much thicker and deeper on his hands than on his twenty-four-year-old counterpart. I missed these hands. "So I'm the love of your life?"

"You always have been," he says.

He grips my hand in his and I see the adoration in his eyes, so much stronger than it was in 2000. He loves me. He loves me more than I could have thought possible. Except there's one last thing that doesn't make sense to me:

"If I'm the love of your life," I say, "then how come you don't want to marry me? You don't even want to live with me. At our first anniversary dinner, you gave me *earrings*."

"Claudia," he says. "Think about it. The only reason you went back was because you wanted to save me from the evil girl who broke my heart. Would you have gone back if you thought we were going to get married and live happily ever after?"

"Well, why would I have?"

"Exactly," he says. "I'm sorry I lied to you about that. But you see why I did it, right? I *had* to."

"But you told me …" I think back to that anniversary dinner. "You said you *weren't ready*. You sounded like you meant it."

"It's true, I wasn't ready," he says. "I hadn't finished the time machine yet. But I have now. Obviously. And I'm ready."

So … is he saying … what exactly is he saying?

Adam reaches for something on the seat of his chair. He pulls out a blue velvet box. I stare at it, my heart pounding. "What the hell is that?" I gasp.

"Well, it's not earrings," he says quietly.

I blink my eyes, which are filling up with tears.

Adam looks up at me, and I see through his glasses that his eyes are in a similar state. "I wasn't exactly sure when we'd meet and when this would all happen, so I bought it a few weeks after we started dating last year."

"Oh, my God," I whisper.

"Claudia," he begins. "I love you so much. I have loved you since the moment I met you sixteen years ago. I would do anything for you, move heaven and earth, build a time machine, *anything*, just to spend my life with you." He opens up the box and the most beautiful diamond ring I've ever seen sits within. "Will you marry me, Claudia?"

"Yes," I say. "Yes!"

It's almost impossible for him to get the ring on my finger because we're both shaking so much. Amazingly, it's a perfect fit. I used to be the one with all the information about him, but now he's the one who knows me like the back of his hand.

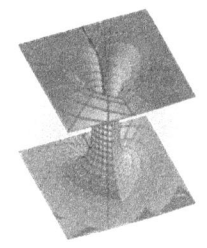

Epilogue

I walk along the outside of Central Park. It's a nice, warm day in September, kind of like the day I first met Adam. I could walk here for hours, just enjoying the breeze and the feel of my sandals against the pavement. But I only have another half hour left. Not much time to mess around.

It takes me another five blocks, but I finally see them and feel a rush of relief. It's a sweet old couple, the kind where you look at them and go "aw." She's got short old-lady hair, dyed honey blond, and arthritic fingers that hold her husband's hand, but she isn't in such bad shape for her age. He's got tufts of thinning white hair and glasses that are far too big for his face, and the lines on his face make him look at least ninety, even though his eyes seem much younger. Also, he's in a wheelchair.

I see them before they see me. I think about sneaking away unnoticed, but the old man's eyes are like a hawk. He nudges his wife and says to her, "There she is!"

I approach them, nervous but admittedly excited. They're both watching me with identical, mildly amused expressions on their faces. They do say after a number of years together, couples start to look alike.

"I told you so," the old man says to me.

I duck my head and smile to myself. Then the old woman gestures to me and I come closer to her so that she can whisper in my ear with her slightly scratchy voice: "You'll throw up when you get back. But it won't be from the time travel."

I grip my abdomen, staring at her. She smiles at me and nods.

That's when I start to hear the now familiar whooshing noise. I quickly scale the gate to get into the park and duck behind a bush so that nobody can see me when I disappear.

When I return to 2014, landing unsteadily on my step with that familiar sense of vertigo, I look up and see Adam sitting there, watching me. He's got little Albert on his lap, who has turned out to be the clingiest rabbit there ever was.

Albert has gotten to like me too, but he really adores Adam—at least as much as a rabbit is capable of adoration. "Well?" Adam says to me.

I smile at him. "We live happily ever after."

"Told you so," he says triumphantly as he leans in to kiss me.

I'm not going to tell him quite yet about the other secret, the one my older self decided to share with me. For now, I just want to enjoy knowing that Adam and I will have our happy ending. I think we earned it.

Annabelle Costa is a teacher, who writes in her free time. She enjoys the wounded hero genre, involving male love interests with physical disabilities, who don't follow the typical Hollywood perception of sexy.

The Boy Next Door

One

I wasn't too happy when my parents told me that I had to try to make friends with the crippled kid who just moved in next door.

I was eight years old. For my entire life thus far, living in a suburb of Pittsburgh, our next door neighbor was an ornery old woman named Agnes. Why are all old people named Agnes, for some reason? Not that I'm prejudiced against old people or anything. My grandmother, Nana, lived with us and was never an ornery old woman, and probably still the best cook I've ever known. Anyway, Agnes failed to wake up one morning, and the house got sold off to a young family with two kids.

I was initially really psyched to find out that the family had two kids, one of whom was allegedly my age. I pictured a girl with blond pigtails who would be my best friend and we'd make each other friendship bracelets, have sleepovers, and all that fun stuff.

But then my fantasy was crushed when I found out that my new eight year old neighbor was a boy. And not just a boy. A boy in a wheelchair.

His name was Jason and I saw him a few

times from afar. He went to a different school than I did, and there was a special school bus that picked him up. I saw him waiting with his parents at the curb for the special bus, which was about half the length of the bus that picked me up. My parents told me it was a bus for disabled kids. When it arrived, a ramp would be lowered mechanically and Jason would wheel into it, and the driver would help him get arranged in the bus. My mother yelled at me not to stare, but how could I not stare?

When the Foxes had been living next door for a few weeks, we came over for a visit and to bring them a welcome basket.

My little sister Lydia and I were dressed up in uncomfortable pink clothes, and I was firmly instructed to play with Jason. Lydia, who was only four, was totally off the hook since the older Fox child was a 13 year old boy.

"I don't want to play with Jason," I whined, as my mother did up the buttons on my dress. "He's weird."

"Oh, stop it," my mother said. "He's not weird."

"He's in a wheelchair," I pointed out.

"Don't you dare mention that," my mother snapped.

"Why not?" spoke up my Nana, who was listening in. "I'm sure the boy knows he's in a wheelchair. It's not a secret, is it?"

Despite everything, I giggled. I wished my mother would let Nana come along, but they were too worried about her making a comment like that. Apparently, she lost her self-censor somewhat as she got older, although Daddy said she'd always kind of been like that.

Fifteen minutes later, my mother was shoving Lydia and me in the direction of the house next door. We rang the bell and Mrs. Fox answered, greeting us warmly. "Jill!" she cried. "I'm so glad you could make it."

"This is for you," my mother said, handing over the basket of fruit and muffins. "You met my husband, Gerald. And these are my daughters, Lydia and Tasha."

"Nice to meet you, girls," Mrs. Fox said. "My older son Randy isn't here now, but Jason is very excited to meet you."

My eyes met those of the boy sitting in a small, simple wheelchair several yards behind his mother. I could tell by his khaki slacks and lame sweater-vest that he too had been forced to dress up for the occasion. He looked just as miserable as I did.

"He's eight, isn't he?" Mom asked. "Tasha is eight as well."

"Yes, that's wonderful," Mrs. Fox said. "They could play together." She lowered her voice to a stage whisper that people a mile away could hear loud and clear: "Jason hasn't been having an easy time making new friends."

Yeah. What a shock.

With that sentiment, Jason and I were herded off in the direction of his bedroom, presumably for me to be his new best friend. We both went, sort of like lambs being led to the slaughter.

Once we were alone in Jason's room, we both just sat there awkwardly, not saying anything to each other. We were too young to even know how to make polite conversation.

I tried not to stare at Jason, but it was hard not to. I mean, really hard. Why did he need a wheelchair anyway? Maybe he had some awful disease where he was dying. Maybe it was contagious! Maybe he had some contagious fatal disease and my mother had locked me alone in a room with him. She'd be so sorry when I died.

Although to be honest, Jason didn't really look like he was dying. He looked pretty much like a normal kid, but he was sitting in a wheelchair. He had short brown hair that it looked like his mother had attempted to comb yet he'd managed to get it messy again before our arrival. He had green eyes that were bright, even in spite of how clearly miserable he was at the moment. And then there were the freckles that were sprinkled down either side of his nose, although those disappeared years later.

I was perched gingerly on Jason's bed. He

had Star Wars blankets. Actually, I had to admit, he had some pretty cool toys.

My mother always bought me dolls, but the thing is, dolls didn't do much. Maybe these days, dolls cry and piss their diapers or whatever, but back then, in the eighties, dolls were much less interesting. But Jason had toys that did cool stuff. He had toy cars and trucks, he had a rocket, and a huge box of Legos. But what really piqued my interest was that he had what looked like a huge box of TRANSFORMERS.

Confession time: I loved Transformers. I watched the TV show religiously every Saturday, rooting for the Autobots to defeat the evil Decepticons. But nobody would buy me any Transformers because I was a girl and obviously it's not an appropriate toy for girls. So I had about half a dozen My Little Ponies and at least a dozen Barbie dolls, but no cars that turned into robots. It was a source of frustration for me. Every time I asked my mother, she'd say, "What do you want one of those awful toys for? You're a girl!"

But Jason, he owned the mother lode.

"Um," I said, working up my nerve. "Are those, um, Transformers?"

Jason brightened. "Yeah. You like Transformers?"

I nodded shyly.

To my delight, Jason grabbed the whole

big box and dumped them out on his bed. He seriously had every Transformer in existence. He had Optimus Prime, of course, most of the Autobots, Megatron, the Decepticons including the cassette spies, plus a bunch of the newer ones like the Dinobots, the Insecticons, and even Devastator. I was majorly impressed. If I were a little older, I would have creamed myself or something.

"Oh my god," I breathed. "You're the luckiest person alive."

Jason grinned. "Wanna play with them?"

I nodded eagerly.

I would say that Jason's knowledge of the Transformers was possibly better than mine, and he even clued me in to the exciting news that this summer *Transformers: The Movie* would be coming out, and would take place in the year 2005, which seemed almost ridiculously futuristic back then. Two hours later, when my parents were ready to go home, they had to literally drag me out of Jason's room, only quieting my whining when they promised to let me come back the next day.

Strangely enough, I got my wish: I became best friends with my next door neighbor. A boy, of all things. I played at Jason's house practically every day after school that year and when the summer came, we went to see the Transformers movie together and were collectively blown away. (I saw it again years later and thought it was the most god awful stupid thing I'd ever seen in my life.) Jason, whose father was a surgeon and spoiled him a little because of his disability, always had the newest and best toys. He even got a small television for his room with a VCR! Jason and I would beg his mom to take us to the video store and rent movies to watch in his room.

We even had sleepovers. I know what you're thinking: a little boy and a girl having a sleepover is weird. But actually, nobody seemed that concerned. After all, we were only eight years old and even though we had the anatomy, we had no idea what to do with it. Plus I get the feeling that the fact that Jason was in wheelchair kind of desexualized him in the minds of our parents. A crippled boy couldn't possibly be lusting after any little girls. The only person who ever questioned it was Nana.

"You're really going to let Tasha spend a night alone with a boy?" Nana asked my mother in amazement.

"It's okay," Mom said. "It's just Jason. The boy in the wheelchair."

"You know, his wiener might not work, but I bet his tongue still does."

"Nana!" Mom cried, glancing at me nervously. "Will you stop it? They're only eight years old!"

Fortunately, I was allowed to go, despite Nana's warnings. Jason's mother helped him change into pajamas in the bathroom, which is how I figured out that he couldn't dress himself, at least back then. He was able to transfer himself into bed, but his mother looked on nervously. It was pretty clear we weren't going to be sneaking to the kitchen to raid the refrigerator at any point that night.

I watched as Jason arranged his legs on the bed as I snuggled into my sleeping bag. I lay staring at the ceiling for a few minutes before I decided I couldn't take it another minute. "Why can't you walk?" I asked, finally verbalizing the question that was in my head for months.

"I was in a car accident when I was five," he told me. "I can't move or feel my legs."

"Oh my gosh!" I exclaimed. "You can't feel them at all?"

Jason shook his head. "It's not a big deal. I'm used to it."

I looked at Jason's feet, knocking together slightly from their position at the end of the bed. On a whim, I reached out and grabbed his ankle. "So you can't feel me touching you?"

"No," he said.

My hand traveled up his leg to his knee. "How about here?"

"No," he said again. He held his hand up to his mid-chest. "Nothing below here."

My eyes widened and I said the first thing that popped into my eight year old head: "So how do you know when you need to go to the bathroom?"

Jason's face turned bright red. "I…" he stammered. "I just…" His voice trailed off, never answering my question. Actually, I think I really didn't want to know the answer to my own question. And I was kind of relieved when he covered his legs back up with his Star Wars blanket.

***

Jason managed to make some friends of his own over the next several years, more gender-appropriate ones, but we remained best friends. After all, he still had the best toys. And he was located very conveniently next door.

When I was eleven and in middle school, I grew breasts. It happened pretty quickly, practically overnight it felt like. One day I had these tiny little mosquito bites on my chest and the next, bam: breasts. I'm not going to lie: I was attractive to guys. I had blond hair and a cute face and now breasts, all of which contributed to a significant popularity with boys. "This one's going to be trouble," Nana used to say practically every day. On my second week of middle school, I was asked out by an older boy at school, a really cute guy named Steve who was universally thought of as being "cool." I accepted, of course.

I told Jason about my impending date with Steve. My relationship with Jason was 100% nonsexual. To be honest, I wasn't even sure if he could have sex, what with being paralyzed and all, and I sure as hell wasn't going to ask him. I had at least a little bit of tact by now. In any case, he had never shown the slightest bit of interest in me in that way. I hadn't entirely eliminated the possibility that he was gay, but I was pretty sure he wasn't, because any time I brought up how sexy Tom Cruise was, he made a face and barfing noises.

Jason was the only person in whom I felt comfortable confiding how nervous I was about the date. "He's so mature," I said, while we were talking within the confines of his bedroom. "What if we go out and he thinks I'm just a baby?"

"I'm sure that won't happen, Tasha," Jason assured me.

"I've never even kissed a boy," I confessed, even though Jason undoubtedly knew it must be true. "What if I suck at it?"

He laughed. "You won't suck at it."

"How do you know?"

"Why would you?"

I wiped my palms on my jeans. They were perpetually sweaty lately. I had never been so nervous about anything in my life. Math tests suddenly seemed entirely insignificant.

"Maybe I should practice?" I suggested.

Jason frowned. "Like on your pillow?"

"No, like, for real," I said. "We could practice together."

Jason's eyes widened and I wondered again if maybe he was gay. "I don't think…"

"Come on, it would really help me," I begged him.

I hadn't really thought this out, but Jason and I were best friends, so it seemed like an obvious thing for best friends to help each other out with. Way better experience than kissing a pillow or my hand. Anyway, it wouldn't be that bad having to kiss Jason. He wasn't gross or anything, like some guys. Not as cute as Steve, obviously, but not bad looking.

"Well, um…" Jason scratched his head, making his hair stand up a bit. "I guess if it would really help you…"

"Awesome!" I clasped my hands together excitedly.

I couldn't help but notice that Jason's cheeks were a little pink. "So, um, what do you want me to do?"

"Well…" I thought about it a minute. "I guess just you sit there and I'll sit on your bed and we'll just… do it."

I put my hands on Jason's shoulders. His green eyes were still wide and I was pretty sure you were supposed to close your eyes to kiss, but then again, I was the one with the date coming up and needed to practice, not him. I leaned in toward him and pressed my lips against his. He barely moved, so I had to do most of the work. His lips were soft and I slipped my tongue inside his mouth. We kissed for, I don't know, thirty seconds or so.

"How was that?" I asked him when I pulled away.

"Um," he said. "That was…fine."

"Just fine?" I asked, disappointed.

Jason shrugged, but when he pulled at his collar, I noticed his hands were shaking.

"Can we try again?"

Jason and I spent the better part of thirty minutes kissing. I think I got better at it, and moreover, it seemed like he got better at it too. He didn't just sit there motionless, he actually moved his tongue in my mouth and put his hands on my shoulders and back. I actually think he was doing a pretty good job towards the end.

Unfortunately, when we were mid lip lock, his mother did her usual knock-and-immediately-enter routine. I could see her mouth fall open when she saw us and Jason's face turned red like a beet. "Mom," he gasped. "Tasha has a date coming up and we were just practicing so…"

Even though it was entirely innocent, needless to say, we weren't allowed to have any more sleepovers after that.

In high school, Jason and my paths diverged even further, though we were finally at the same school. I really embraced the whole grunge look, dating guys with long messy hair and ripped jeans. I actually cried when Kurt Cobain died and I tried my damnedest to look as much like Courtney Love as I could manage. I wore ripped fishnet stockings and way, way too much eye make-up. I mean, at the time, it seemed like the right amount of eye make-up, but in retrospect I'm majorly embarrassed.

Jason, on the other hand, descended into geekdom. He had a computer before anyone else I knew and he spent an unhealthy amount of time on that thing. His friends were the biggest pimple-faced losers in the school. He committed further social suicide by joining math team and then even something called the Computer Club. If he was anyone else, I wouldn't have been caught dead with him. As it was, we barely talked while we were at school.

When we were about fifteen years old, I came by Jason's room to hang out and he was wearing glasses. I gasped in horror. "Take those off!" I cried. "Come on, you look like a total nerd! You don't really need those, do you?"

Jason raised his eyebrows at me. "Um, yeah, I do."

"That's because you spend too much time

on the computer," I said.

"You're probably right," he said, and pulled off the lenses. He didn't look that bad with them, I guess, but it was really hard to keep Jason from turning into a complete nerd. He just didn't seem to get it. Or care. But that didn't stop me from making an effort.

"That's better," I said. "After all, how are you going to get a girlfriend wearing those?"

Jason just laughed. As far as I knew, he'd never had a date. I was pretty sure he was straight because I once found some issues of Playboy stuffed into his pillowcase, but he seemed totally unconcerned with his dateless status. I guess he figured that being a geek in a wheelchair wasn't likely to land him a date.

I sat cross-legged on Jason's bed and rolled a joint. He went through his drawer and pulled out a lighter and tossed it to me. I took a deep drag and handed the joint to Jason, who took an impressive drag of his own. He blinked and I could almost see his eyes turning bloodshot. "Ah, Tasha," he muttered. "You get the best weed."

"As if any of your loser friends could score you weed," I retorted, slugging him gently in the shoulder.

"You're right, Tash," he said. "What would I do without you?"

I have to admit, there were few people I had as much fun getting high with as Jason. He was one of the few people I felt I could really be myself around, maybe the only person. Plus his parents didn't get home from work till totally late and gave us more than enough time to clear out the smell of the pot.

Despite being a picture of teen angst, I still wanted to go to our senior prom. The hottest guy in our class asked me to be his date (under the assumption that he'd get a little post-prom action... I was not exactly chaste). I even picked out a black dress at the local department store that flattered my figure and made my (now quite large) breasts look amazing.

I didn't even have to ask Jason if he intended to go to prom. I was 99.9% sure he hadn't asked a girl out during all of high school, so I doubted he had managed to get himself a prom date. I guessed he was going to spend prom night on the computer, chatting online with his other nerdy buddies. It bothered me to think about that. Jason was cute and he was a great guy—he deserved to get a date. So what if he was a bit of a geek and he was disabled? Those were qualities that could be overlooked, at least for one night.

"Forget it, Tasha," Jason said to me when I brought it up to him. "The only way I'm going to have a date for prom is if I go with my mom."

"Oh, stop it," I said. "There are tons of girls who would go out with you."

Jason snorted. "No," he said, "there aren't."

"You're selling yourself short."

"I'm realistic. I mean, look at me."

I gave Jason a quick once over, trying to see him from the eyes of a girl who hadn't been best friends with him for the past ten years. He had good qualities, speaking objectively. His short hair was always adorably mussed and he had really vivid green eyes, even though he unfortunately hid them behind glasses all the time these days. From the neck up, he was cute, even very cute. He had this sort of half-smile he gave that was very endearing. And from the times I'd seen him in a T-shirt, I could testify that he had some impressive muscles in his arms. Unfortunately, if the T-shirt didn't fit quite right, I could also see the paunch in his abdomen from muscles that obviously didn't exist anymore.

And when he shifted in his chair, which he did a lot, it was kind of weird the way his legs didn't move on their own. It was a little strange, if you're not used to it. I was used to it. But other girls weren't. And it was probably true that the presence of the chair itself made people uncomfortable.

"What about that girl Sofia?" I suggested. "From the math team?"

"You mean the one who speaks like five words of English?"

"Um, I guess…"

"She's got a date."

"Oh." I bit my lip, thinking through the less desirable members of our class. "What about that girl Chelsea?"

"The one who's autistic?"

"She's not autistic," I protested. "Just… keeps to herself."

"Please, Tasha," he said. "This is getting insulting." He looked at my face and flashed me that half-smile. "It's okay, really. Prom's not a big deal to me. I don't even want to go, to be honest."

"Well, is there any girl that you like?" I asked him. "I mean, you're not gay, right?"

"Christ, Tasha," Jason said, shaking his head.

"Are you?"

"No!"

"Then there must be someone you like," I deduced. I caught Jason's hesitation. "There is! I knew it!"

He bit his lip. "Yeah, well, it doesn't really matter."

"Come on," I said. "You really think a girl would turn you down just because you're in a wheelchair?"

"It doesn't matter why," he said. "I just know for a fact that she would."

He seemed so sure of himself that I didn't even argue with him. "Well, if that's the case," I said, "she's not worth it."

"That," he said, "is definitely debatable."

Prom was basically my life for the next couple of months. I always thought I was the kind of girl who was too cool to be excited about the prom, but there it was. On the night of the dance, Nana volunteered to help me get into my dress. She had gotten older, but still had as much energy as ever. "I'd tell you not to have sex tonight," she said, "but I know it's a lost cause."

I didn't say anything, just smiled at my reflection in the full length mirror. I looked hot.

"So who's the lucky guy?" Nana asked me. "You going with that Fox boy from next door? The crippled one? You certainly spend enough time with him."

"Jason?" I turned to look at Nana in surprise. Usually she was pretty perceptive about stuff. "You know he and I are just friends."

"Sure," Nana said.

"We are!" I insisted.

"Uh huh," Nana said. "And I'd bet your inheritance that the boy thinks about you and only you when he pleasures himself."

"Nana!" I blushed under my make-up. "He does not! We don't feel that way about each other. We've known each other too long."

Nana shrugged. "Believe what you want, Natasha."

I felt a moment of hesitation. But really, I

was pretty sure Jason wasn't in love with me. I would have known if he felt that way about me. I'd have sensed it. Anyway, even if he did, there was nothing I could do about it now.

I had a great time at prom. My date made me the envy of pretty much every girl in the room, then afterwards I gave him what I promised in the men's room. He even drove me home, and told me he'd call me, even though I wasn't dumb enough to think he would.

I didn't go straight home though. I had an hour left on my prom night curfew so instead I went next door and knocked on Jason's first floor window. I peered inside and saw he was in bed. With the lights out. He sat up in bed as I shimmied the window open. "Are you burglarizing me?" he asked.

"Why?" I retorted. "You got anything worth stealing?"

"Well, you've had your eye on my Nintendo for years…"

I laughed. Jason rubbed his eyes and smiled at me. He looked adorably sleepy. I remembered what Nana said about him earlier in the night and decided she had to be mistaken. "I take it you had a good time?"

I nodded eagerly. "I wish you had been there."

"Isn't it better this way?" he asked, smiling. "This way you get to tell me about it."

I laughed again because he was absolutely right. I wanted nothing more than to recount every minute of my fantastic evening to my best friend. He listened dutifully as I sat perched at the edge of his bed, giving him an animated account of the night until the time was up on my curfew and I snuck back out the window and went home.

Jason, the smart bastard, got into Yale for college, while I ended up at the city college, living at home. The first two years of college, we emailed each other nearly constantly. Although Jason wasn't introverted or anything, he had a lot of trouble making friends due to his disability. He did make friends, but they were the same type of loser guy computer geeks he hung out with in high school. But the difference was that while in high school, he had accepted his status as perpetually dateless, now that he was in college, he was talking about girls more and more. I could hear him getting frustrated. My heart went out to him.

Then one day during our junior year, he emailed me that a girl named Sally in his computation theory class had accepted a dinner invitation. I imagined that Sally, a computer science major, was hideously ugly and probably had a moustache or something, yet I found myself feeling... well, I'm not sure if jealous is the right word, but... I don't know. Every time Jason mentioned Sally in an email, I'd feel myself cringe. Even though he continued to respond quickly to all my emails, I felt like I had lost my desire to keep in touch with him. Eventually, it just seemed like so much effort to keep writing to my (former) best friend. So I stopped. No explanation, no apology… I just stopped writing to him.

After college, I got the hell out of Pittsburgh and moved to New York City. I had taught myself to play the electric guitar in college and I agreed to front a band called (much to my current embarrassment) Cynthia's Armpit. I'm mortified by the band name now, but at the time it seemed impossibly cool, as did the guys in the band, which is why I had fucked pretty much all of them within a month's time.

I used to describe Cynthia's Armpit as an edgier version of the band Garbage. I thought of myself as a young Shirley Manson (who was probably actually not that much older than me) and even dyed my hair red to emulate her. You can imagine that Cynthia's Armpit was not a raging success. We got a few gigs playing bars and coffee shops, usually for no payment except free drinks, and sometimes not even that. I supported myself by waitressing.

When I think of how I used to get up there in front of huge crowds dressed in slutty, skintight outfits, my eyes caked in black make-up, shouting out lyrics because I couldn't really sing... well, it's not something I like to go around telling people. But at the time, I totally thought I was The Shit.

One night, a couple of years into the band's trajectory toward failure, Cynthia's Armpit was playing at some seedy bar in the village. It was the kind of bar where I had to take a trench coat with me to immediately drape around myself so I didn't get raped the second I got off the stage. But within the crowd of would-be rapists watching me sing, I saw one guy who seemed incredibly out of place.

The guy was wearing a suit and tie, for one thing, rather than a wife-beater T-shirt. The suit looked expensive too. It was hard to see him due to the lighting in the bar, but he seemed really cute too, if a bit too clean cut. I could see him bobbing his head to our cacophonous music and I was pleased that a cute, well dressed guy was digging us. Or maybe just digging me. I hadn't dated a cute, successful guy in... well, ever.

As soon as our set was over, I put away my guitar in its case and went over to say hello to the mysterious stranger. But before his face became clear from within the shadows of the bar, I saw the wheels on the ground below him and my heart leapt. As I got closer and saw those bright green eyes behind the rimless frames, I realized I wasn't looking at stranger. "Jason?" I said in amazement. "What are you doing here?"

He flashed that endearing half-grin. "Well, I came to listen to the great Tasha Moran sing, of course."

I couldn't help myself—I threw my arms around him in a great big bear hug, which he returned with equal eagerness. The hug lasted like five minutes, I was so happy to see him. When it was finally over, I dropped into the chair next to him. "It's so good to see you!" I sighed. "How did you find me?"

He shrugged. "Our mothers live next door to each other. It wasn't hard. Cynthia's Armpit is the kind of name that bears repeating."

I blushed. "I know. It seemed so cool at first, but now…"

"I like it," Jason said. "You just need to make sure to copyright it before someone steals it."

I slugged him in the arm. "Oh my god, shut up!"

Jason grinned at me. "It's good to see you too, Tash. Love the red hair."

"It's not too red?" I asked self-consciously. Yesterday I'd been at Macy's and some old woman was shaking her head at me disapprovingly. A few years ago, I would have thrived on a look like that, but now it was beginning to bother me.

"Hair can never be too red, can it?" Jason asked, smiling. "Anyway, you can pull it off."

I looked him up and down, confirming that his suit was as expensive as it appeared from afar. "You look like you're doing well."

He pulled at his tie. "Investment banking. I know, don't say it."

"Say what?"

"That I've sold out to corporate America to make money."

"I wasn't going to say that."

"Well, you'd be the first," Jason said. "But this is all part of my plan to retire at forty and then do something really worthwhile."

"Like what?"

"Christ, I don't know," he said. "Open an orphanage? Rescue lost puppies? I'm only 25, I've got some time to think about it."

As Jason loosened his tie again with his left hand, I couldn't help but notice the lack of a ring on his fourth finger. He wasn't married. Actually, I was surprised. Despite his failure with girls in high school, I had always thought he'd meet some girl in college, fall head over heels for her, and they'd get hitched after graduation. Part of the reason I stopped writing to him was that I didn't know if I wanted to hear about it when it happened. Not that I didn't want Jason to be happy, because I did. But I felt like losing my best friend to another woman would be more than I could handle. It was easier to give him up voluntarily first.

"So," Jason said, "are you done for the night? Can I buy you a drink?"

Our eyes met and for a moment, it was very clear that he hadn't come here for the sake of friendship. My heart leaped in my chest as I contemplated my answer, but before I could say anything, our drummer Sonny plopped down next to me and threw a hand around my shoulder. Then, to make matters worse, he planted a big sloppy kiss on the corner of my mouth.

"Hey, Tasha," Sonny said. "This guy bothering you?"

"No," I said quickly, as Sonny started flexing his tattooed biceps. "This is my, um, old friend Jason."

"Cool," Sonny said. He held out his hand and Jason shook it. "I'm Sonny, Tasha's boyfriend."

Sonny's statement wasn't entirely false. We were sleeping together (and he gave me Chlamydia, thank you very much) and occasionally we had dinner or hit a party or club together. So I couldn't really deny it. Especially since Cynthia's Armpit was going through some inner turmoil recently and I didn't want to do anything to upset the balance further.

"Oh," Jason said. He seemed slightly taken

aback, but recovered quickly. "Well, it's nice to meet you."

"We've got to go back on in five," Sonny said, running a hand over his shaved head. He wanted people to think he was Michael Stipe, but really, he was just hiding his thinning hair.

"Don't let me keep you, Tasha," Jason said quickly. He glanced down at his watch. "I've got an early meeting tomorrow and I actually kind of need to head out soon."

As I looked at Jason's familiar face, I knew I couldn't let him out of my life again. "Let me give you my cell number," I said. "We could, um, have lunch sometime."

Jason smiled. "That would be great. I'll call you this weekend." And he programmed my number into his phone.

Jason backed away from his table and wheeled toward the door as we were setting up our instruments again. Sonny's eyes widened when he saw Jason's exit. "Holy shit," he said. "I didn't realize that guy was crippled. I thought he was hitting on you or something."

"No," I said quietly, feeling a twinge of regret. "We're just old friends."

As promised, Jason called me that weekend and we had lunch on Sunday. We caught up on old times, but nothing more. Somehow if there had been a chance for Jason and I to be more than friends, the opportunity had passed us by. But that lunch succeeded in rekindling our lost friendship, and within a few months, Jason had been promoted back to Best Friend, a status he has retained to this day.

Which made it only fitting that he should be the one throwing my 32nd birthday party.